BED OF ROSES

BED OF ROSES

BOUQUET OF LIES DUET
Book One

USA TODAY BESTSELLING AUTHOR
DV FISCHER

LN
♡P

PLAYLIST

Lay Me Down by The Band Perry
Wolves by Down Like Silver
Hells Comin With Me by Poor Man's Poison
Lose Control by Teddy Swims
Spite by Vandaveer
Ain't No Sunshine by Shawn James
Never Tear us Apart by Bishop Briggs
Hellfire by Barns Courtney

Are you scared, sweetheart? You should be.

— YOUR BOOK BOYFRIEND, COLE
GARNER

BED OF ROSES

CHAPTER 1
TEGAN ADAMS

"**D**o you think this is what's best?" Dr. Lynn asked. I could tell he was doing that reverse psychology thing that he loved to use so much. Although it has been proven useful in the past, it won't work on me this time.

"I need to. For me, I have to leave," I answered as I grabbed my purse from the base of the couch.

"Your parents just died a few days ago, Tegan."

"I know. I was there." I stood and held out my hand to shake his for the final time. There would be no returning to therapy. At least, not in Chicago.

He stood with me, his expression open and pleading. Somewhere in the background, a clock dinged; our session had officially begun. But I only came to say goodbye.

"Making rash decisions in the moment of grief is normal, but—"

"It's not rash if I'm drowning. The only way to stop drowning is to get out of the water, Dr. Lynn." I

*dropped my hand and shouldered my purse.
"Goodbye."*

*He rubs his fingers over his goatee, and I don't
wait for any other protests before I'm out the door.*

"Jesus. Shit," I grumble as my car jostles me
around, thanks to a particularly nasty pothole.

This part of Utah is nearly abandoned. It's in the
middle of nowhere. With a town of less than two thousand people, it sure feels like it anyway. And with
roads such as these—riddled with potholes and no
visible center and shoulder lines—it's a miracle those
two thousand people have stuck around.

Maples and firs hug the road, and up ahead, above
the tree line, I can see the tips of subtle mountains.
Thanks to summer, everything is lush green, and the
birds swoop across the road to nestle in branches on
the other side.

It's a far cry from Chicago, where the tallest thing
in the city was a man-made building that always
blotted out the sun. Here, I don't even share the road
with anyone. The only shadows are from the trees and
the puffy white clouds that occasionally give a
reprieve from the hot beams.

Still, even with the unfamiliarity, I'm glad Tori
talked me into this. Well, she didn't need to do much
convincing. When my parents died, I was ready to
leave. I had nothing left for me, and I wanted more
than anything to run away from the life I carried.
Besides, I was a grown-ass woman. I can run if I want
to, despite Dr. Lynn's warnings not to.

As soon as I see the mailbox with the faded
address number I've been searching for etched haphaz-

ardly on it, I turn into the gravel driveway, relieved that I've finally made it to my destination. The driveway winds around the trees, and just like the road, the gravel drive has seen better days. Derek Wordon, the man whom I'm renting this property from, said that it needed some work, but hopefully, the house is in better shape than the driveway.

My heart sinks when the house comes into view, however. "Wow," I whisper in both awe and disgust.

I pull up to the one-story house, park beside a rusted truck, and shut my car off. The house is definitely worse than the driveway. The siding is wood, and the white paint is peeling off of it in layers like skin from a bad sunburn. It has a broken front window that's taped off with what looks to be a plastic trash bag, and what was once surely a beautiful rock garden is now wild and beastly, unidentifiable growth.

"At least the roof looks new," I say to myself as I adjust my shirt over my wide stomach. I agreed to help fix the place up in exchange for cheaper rent, but I don't know a damn thing about shingles.

I swivel my gaze to the rest of the property. Off to the right, squatting in the overgrown grass, I spot a metal shed. To the right of that is a barn that's leaning to the side.

Stepping out of my car, I stand with the door hanging open, shielding my eyes as I squint past the shed and the barn. "Are those horses?" I whisper to myself. I hope I'm not expected to take care of them. Like shingles, I wouldn't know what to do with them.

Keeping the horses in the pasture is a barbed wire fence that extends into the grove of maples at the top of the slight hill. But that's not what pulls my attention. Inside the fence is a large patch of roses. From here, I can see their bright red buds in full bloom, but just like the rest of the property, they haven't been kept. The roses grow wild, pushing against the barbed wire that keeps them in and the horses out.

Hinges squeak. "Ms. Adams?"

I turn my head to the higher-pitched male voice, owner of the man now waiting in the house's doorway, and paste on a smile so fake that it hurts my cheeks. I shut my car door. "Mr. Wordon?"

He steps fully out of the house, and the screen door slams shut behind him. "How many times do I have to tell you? It's Derek."

My smile warms as I cross the tall grass and shake his hand. "I'll only call you by your first name if you use mine."

He puckers his lips as if it takes much thought to consider. "Tegan it is then."

"That's all I ask," I say brightly as I give his hand one last squeeze before releasing his fingers and letting him go.

He chuckles a little, and it's so girly that I can't help but laugh with him.

Derek is not a handsome man. He's thin with absolutely no muscle mass. On top of his head is a severe balding spot that he brushes hair from the side up and over to hide, and he wears glasses too big for his small face. The glasses make his nose look much larger than it really is. But he seems nice, and I couldn't give a shit what he looks like. He was kind enough to rent me this dump, and for a good price too, considering I'm between jobs.

"I hope your travels went well."

I nod and look back at the car that made the long haul. "We managed."

"Good. Good." He pauses, and I glance back at him. "Chicago, huh?"

"Yep," I answer, pocketing my hands in my jeans pockets. "Born and raised."

A tiny frown furrows his bushy eyebrows. "If you don't mind me asking, why Fairview, Utah?"

I shrug a little. "My best friend moved here after college. She offered me a job." And a way to escape, but I keep that to myself. He doesn't need to know all the details. It'd probably frighten him off, and I really need this place to stay, even if it might be infested by termites. In such a remote area, there weren't many places to rent.

"It's a small town, Tegan. Everyone knows everyone here, so color me curious when I ask who your friend is."

"Tori Townsend."

"Ah, the realtor."

I nod. "She also owns a metaphysical shop in Mount Pleasant. She's almost ready to open it."

He smiles a small smile. "Interesting. I hadn't heard. She's a restless one, that one. I'm surprised she's stuck around for as long as she has."

My grin widens as I agree with him. "She said she'd never get tired of the mountains." She complains about the lack of available booty calls, though.

"Fair enough," he says, stepping aside and

sweeping his arm out. "Well, welcome home. It ain't much, but I'm sure you and Cole will have it fixed up in no time."

"Cole?" I ask, scowling. I had assumed all this work would be me and many self-help videos.

He puckers his lips again. "Did I forget to tell you about the handyman?"

I rub at my eyebrow. I was hoping for solitude, but now I'll have some strange man running around my space, making constant noises and endless messes. "Yeah. Yeah, you did."

"I hope you don't mind. It's just too big of a project for one person to handle."

I drop my hand back down and try not to flatten my lips. "Totally fine, Derek. We will make it work."

"Great to hear." He bows his head in approval. "Are you ready to see the inside?"

"Sure," I say chipperly.

Together, we start to walk toward the door. "Now, this isn't a palace by any means. It hasn't had anyone living in it for over a year."

"A renter?" I ask because perhaps the previous renter destroyed the place. It's not unheard of. They definitely didn't maintain it. Or maybe that's Derek's fault.

"My brother, actually. Not a renter." He glances at me from over his shoulder for a second. "It was his place. He inherited it from our parents with the hopes of fixing it up, back to its original glory."

"Did he decide against it?" I press as he pauses with his hand on the door handle. I could totally see someone looking at this and thinking it was too much work and just walking away.

"He-uh—" He pushes his glasses up with his free hand, hiding the pinch of his eyebrows as he looks down at my neck. "He disappeared a year ago."

"Oh," I whisper. I can tell there's more to that story, but by his expression, he doesn't want to be forthcoming with information. So instead, I touch his shoulder. "I'm sorry."

He shrugs, and the hinges squeal as he opens the screen door. "Anyway, the place is mine now. That's all you need to worry about."

He steps inside as a waft of dust and mold stuffs its way up my nose. *Oh boy.* I brace myself and follow him inside. My eyes adjust to the darkness of the space, and I almost wish they wouldn't.

The front door leads to the living room. The first thing my eyes zoom to is the cobwebs in every crevice. The meager sun shining through the gritty windows reflects on them, announcing their presence in each corner, across the faded dark green couch and matching recliner. A fireplace sits on one wall, but I don't think it's been cleaned since the house was built. Black soot crawls up the sides of the brick, and a generous pile of ash squats at the bottom.

In the corner is a grand piano. I've never played myself, but I do like the sound of a good melody.

I take a step deeper inside, and my foot creaks against the hardwood floors. I look down at my feet. The toes of my tennis shoes are touching a large black rug that crawls across the entire space. "Original floors?" I ask. Because what the hell else am I going to say?

"Sure is!" he exclaims proudly. Directly after, he goes into a fit of coughs.

I wait until he's done to nod and venture deeper into the living room. I brush my hand against the back of the couch, careful to avoid the cobwebs. My fingertips grit against the dust on the fabric, but my eyes take in the space better.

On the yellowing floral wallpapered walls are pictures that were probably Derek's parents. I head to one and brush my finger against the glass protecting the picture to remove the dust and get a better look. It's a family of five and so old that the picture is faded and even more yellow than the wallpaper.

"Is this you?" I ask, gesturing vaguely to the picture. In the photograph, there are three boys, an older, middle-aged woman, and a hunched, over-worked man. The boys look to be in their teens.

Derek crosses the living room and squints at the picture. He points to one teen and says, "This is me." His finger moves to the other two. "This is my brother Neil, the one who disappeared, and this is my step-brother George. He's the sheriff now." He glances at me conspiratorially. "My father remarried when my real mother died. She came with a son."

I get the distinct feeling that Derek wasn't a fan of adding another brother to his family. "Did you all get along?" I ask as I head to the other pictures. Most are hunting photographs.

He laughs. "No. Well, George and Neil did, but I would have been better off as an only child."

I grin at that. I have no siblings myself, but I never wanted any. I can see his point.

Above the hearth is a deer head with antlers for days. I head to it, frown, and poke the nose. This will be the first thing that goes, I decide immediately. I walked away from death when I left Chicago. I don't need it here, either, even if it is just a trophy.

"Do you want to see the rest of the house?" Derek asks.

I swivel and nod. "Love to."

He waves me on and heads down a hallway. "There are two bedrooms."

"It must have been hell, sharing a bedroom with two brothers," I observe as I follow him.

"You have no idea," he grumbles as he opens one bedroom. "This is the master. You'll be pleased to know that there's an adjoining bathroom."

I head inside and take in the space. Cobwebs hang throughout here too, but, like the living room, it's fully furnished as promised. I hadn't brought anything from my Chicago apartment. In fact, I sold it all for the money to move out here.

The bed is queen-sized and covered with a hand-made quilt made out of old jeans. The bedding will be the first thing I wash. Who knows when the last time was that it had seen water and soap?

In the corner, beside the window, sits a cheval mirror layered in dust, and along the wall beside it is a large dresser. There's no closet, but I don't keep fancy clothes that need to be hung. I'm not that kind of girl.

Nothing hangs on the walls except one picture. From a quick glance, and from seeing the teenage version of him in the living room, I can deduce that it's a picture of Derek's missing brother. It's a little weird to have a random picture of yourself, but okay.

To the right of the dresser is another door, so I open it and peek into the bathroom, withholding a groan. Everything is pale pink: the tiled countertops, the sink, the toilet, the shower. "Wow," is all I say.

"Yeah, it needs some work," he murmurs from the hallway. "But everything works, I assure you."

"The plumbing too?" I ask as I shut the door to the offending bathroom and turn back to face Derek.

"Cole has redone all the plumbing and fixed all the electrical already," he says proudly.

I nod a little. "Is this house his only project?" Because honestly, if it isn't, I know that I'll be doing the majority of this work.

"Yes," he divulges. He starts coughing into the crook of his arm.

I frown and head to him. "Is it the dust?"

He waves me off, his eyes watering. "No, not the dust. The doctors and I aren't sure what it is. But it's of no matter; we'll figure it out. Anyway,"— he waves me off again—"Cole doesn't have any other jobs. No one will hire him."

My eyebrows pull down severely. "Why?" I ask skeptically.

He does that lip-puckering again. Honestly, it's like he's sucking on a lemon. "His stint in prison made him undesirable as hired help. But he sure learned how to fix things up while he was in there."

"An ex-con?" I ask in disbelief.

"Will that be a problem?" he presses, taking in my expression.

"Um—I mean—" I push a stray blond hair behind my ear and tug my shirt down over my belly again. "Is he dangerous?"

"Who, Cole?"

I raise my eyebrows. Were we talking about someone else? Instead of voicing my sarcasm, I nod.

"He's harmless," he says, crossing his arms defensively. "Rough around the edges, but he won't hurt you."

Having to take his word for it, I sigh and step out of the master bedroom. I start to lead the tour and peek into the next bedroom. It's been cleared of the furniture, so I shut the door and take a look in the bathroom directly across the hall from it. Instead of pink, it's all blue. Honestly, what is with these colors? There are absolutely no redeeming qualities in this house, minus the walls holding up the roof.

I turn toward Derek, who had been silently following me. "Kitchen?"

He waves me on, and we head back through the hallway, across the living room, and into what is surely the dining room. Several large windows in the dining room overlook the pasture, maples, and firs. To my surprise, an antique table squats directly in the middle of the room that's riddled with construction tools across the surface. Instead of balking at the mistreatment of a beautiful piece of furniture, I turn to the kitchen, where Derek had already entered.

I rub my shoulder as soon as I step into the

kitchen. The joint is already aching at the prospect of what this kitchen will do to it.

The cabinets are dark wood, and the style is straight from the seventies. The countertop has already been removed, but I can tell it was tiled like the bathroom because it holds a few trashcans full of smashed tiles.

The sink is an old farmhouse sink, and I head to it to run my fingers across its smooth surface. It's in perfect condition, and I find myself giddy about that. It's a little treasure in a place that would be better if it were burned to the ground. "Can we keep this?"

"Sure, just let Cole know."

I breathe a sigh of relief that at least some old charm from the house can stay. Maybe some white paint on the dark cabinets can cheer up the space. "When will the countertops be in?"

He pockets his hands in his back pockets. "That's on order. With us being way out here, it'll take some time. I can have Cole put wood on the counters for now so that you have a surface to cook on."

"That'd be great," I murmur as I head to the stove, and a slow smile spreads across my lips. "The appliances look new."

"Neil had replaced the old ones since they didn't work."

"Wonderful," I say, meaning it. Having working appliances that I'm familiar with will make this a hell of a lot easier on me. Plus, it's several things that I don't have to try and haul out of here because, honestly, I have no faith in an ex-con's work ethic to lend me a hand.

"Well," he says, slapping his thighs. "I'll let you get to it. You have my number, right?"

I turn to him. "Saved it in my phone."

"Great!" he exclaims. It sends him into a coughing fit where he turns away from me to hack up a lung. "Jesus have mercy on me," he grumbles when it's over.

"Are you sure you're okay?"

He waves me off as he turns back to face me, wiping at his eyes. "Cleaning supplies are in the cabinets, and there's a pantry"—he points to a few tall cabinets—"that has the rest of the supplies. A broom, a duster, things of the like."

"Okay, great. And where can I get paint and such?"

"Mount Pleasant." He flicks a thumb over his shoulder. "I have a few charge accounts there. Tori can show you around to get what you need." He clears his throat, and I can tell he's about to go into another coughing fit. "I need to get out of here. I think you're right, and the dust is making it worse."

I give him a reassuring smile and make a shooing motion at him. "I'll let you know if I need anything."

"Please do," he says as he turns and strides out of the kitchen. "I'll get ahold of Cole and let him know you've settled in." Shortly after, I hear the screen door shut.

CHAPTER 2
COLE GARNER

E ven over the TV, I can hear his hacking before he rings the bell. I roll my eyes as the bell echoes throughout my trailer. Well, it's not *my* trailer. I rent it from Derek, one of the few houses he took over from his brother when he died, or disappeared, depending on who you ask in this part of Utah.

I don't answer it right away because maybe if I sit here, he'll think I'm not home. Even though my truck is outside, I could be on a stroll through the neighborhood or some shit like that.

From my lying position on the couch, I can see his outline through the plaid curtain. The curtain is faded and worn. It came with the house, and I've had zero desire to change it. Make it more personalized. That just isn't me, and it's certainly not in the funds. Besides, from what I hear, Derek Wordon is making bank. Good for him. I couldn't give a rat's ass, but I also can't help but overhear shit when I go into town.

This place is full of gossip, worse than prison, and even though I grew up here, I'm still amazed at how much shit people have to say about one another.

It's like they're bored or something. They have no idea what boredom truly is. When they sit in a cell with nothing more than a cellmate, we can discuss what it truly means to be bored.

So, basically, if Derek doesn't like the curtains, he can change them himself. Between him and me, we both know he's too cheap to do that.

He rings the doorbell again.

Suppressing a growl, I set my beer down on the end table, slide my legs off the couch, and head to the door. The door is full of claw marks because the previous tenants had three huskies. I've found the evidence throughout the place since I moved in a few months ago when prison finally let me go. Dog hair. Dug holes. Chewed trim. The works.

Swinging the door open, I watch as Derek, who is wiping the spittle from his mouth with the back of his hand, looks me up and down. I'm wearing nothing but a pair of shorts. This may be his trailer, but it's my home, and if I don't want to change after I work out, I don't have to.

"Did you get those abs in jail?" Derek asks when he raises his frown to me. "I don't remember you having those before you went. You were a scrawny kid."

I grunt. "There wasn't much else to do but lift a few weights."

"I assume that's what you were doing by all the sweat." He gestures vaguely to my body.

15

I look down at my stomach, which shines with perspiration. Yes, before my beer, I was working out, but what the fuck does that have to do with anything? "What do you want, Derek?" I don't pay him rent; it comes out of the work I do for him. I can't think of another reason he'd stop by because surely he learned a long time ago that I've never been the person for a chat. *That* fact infuriated my cellmate, who was compelled to tell me everything about his life, and I refused to tell him anything in return. He knew why I was in—everyone did—but that's all I'd give away. I only told them in hopes that they'd leave me alone, but that didn't deter my cellmate one bit.

"Are you going to invite me in?"

Since I'm several inches taller, I scowl down at him. "Why?"

He matches my scowl until I relent and step aside. Whatever he's here for must be good if he wants to come inside.

I shut the door behind him and watch as he takes in my space. It isn't much. When I went to prison as a teen, I didn't own anything besides the clothes on my back, and I outgrew those a long time ago. Everything I have, I've bought over the last few months thanks to the work I do for Derek.

A couch sits in the middle of the living room and faces a too-small TV. The TV only gets a few sports channels and one news program. Most of the time, I sit with it off.

Beside the couch is the end table with my beer squatting on it. Between the coffee, the protein shakes, and the beers, there are permanent circle marks on the wood surface.

I have no pictures, nothing to give away my interests and hobbies. Not that I have any. I didn't before I went away either. My interests surrounded my sister and making sure she was protected.

Beyond the living room is a kitchen that has the bare minimum of kitchenware. I don't cook, so the freezer is stocked full of frozen dinners, but the fridge at least has fruits, vegetables, and protein drinks.

To the right of the kitchen is a hallway that leads to the only bedroom and bathroom. The bed is second-hand from an estate auction a few towns over. It was probably owned by an old bat who died in her sleep, but I couldn't care less. It's a place to sleep, nothing more.

"Still redecorating, I see," Derek says when he gets his fill of my space.

I grunt again and cross my arms over my chest. "Is that what you came for? To see if I settled in?"

"I have to admit, you not making this homey has me nervous that you're flighty."

I chuckle, drop my arms, and head to my beer. After a swig, I scratch at the stubble of my jaw. "I'm not going anywhere. I just don't see any reason to make it more than what it is."

"And that is?" he presses.

"A roof over my head."

"I see," he comments dryly with a nod. While he heads into a small bout of coughs, I sit on the couch and relax. "Damn this…whatever this is."

"You look like shit, Derek." He does. He's thinner

than he used to be, and it's only been a couple of weeks since I saw him last. Dark circles are starting to appear under his eyes, too. No doubt, if he's coughing like this all the time, he probably isn't sleeping well either.

He clears his throat and rolls his shoulders. "I swear to God, if the doctor doesn't have answers by my next visit…"

"What? You'll fire him?" I ask with humor.

"Well, I'll do something," he answers defensively.

"Mm-hmm," I hum. There aren't many doctors around here to begin with, but I have to admit we had better care in prison than we do in this area. Unless it's basic, he'll never find out what's truly wrong with him. Clearly, it's not basic. He probably has cancer or something, which would suck because, if this man dies, I'm out of a place to live. Not many people would rent to an ex-con. "Have you thought about looking into it yourself?"

"According to search engines, I'm dying," he adds with a roll of his eyes.

"Aren't we all," I grumble around the rim of my beer. We're all going to die someday, but it sounds like, out of the two of us in the room, he'll go first.

"Anyway—" He waves me off. "I'm sure you're wondering why I'm here."

"Since the moment you rang my doorbell."

He raises his eyebrows above the rim of his glasses. "I have a new renter at that house I'm having you fix up."

Pinching the bridge of my nose with my free hand,

I briefly close my eyes. "I told you I didn't want anyone to live there while I worked on it."

"Tough shit. It's not up to you."

"Why?" I look at him squarely with a flex to my jaw that he doesn't miss.

"Because it needs to bring in revenue."

"Always after the money, I see," I comment gruffly.

He narrows his eyes at me. "Screw you, Garner. I don't think you realize how good you have it here."

I roll my eyes. "You and I both know that the only reason you rented this place out to me is to rattle your stepbrother."

He wets his bottom lip, and I almost think he's going to deny it, but then he says, "It was a pleasure to see the look on his face when he found out. I was lucky to be there for that."

Derek told me that his stepbrother found out over tea in his own house. As a way to shove it to Derek, to prove that he's better, his stepbrother always buys his tea for him. It's a pissing contest if you ask me, but Derek won't say no to anything free.

"And you're still not worried that he could make your life a living hell?"

"Why? Because he's the sheriff?" he asks. I nod, and he rocks back on his heels in thought. "He could try."

And he'd probably succeed, I don't say. But as far as I can tell, that bastard George Smith hasn't done anything unsavory in retaliation.

Officer Smith and I don't get along. We have our reasons. Valid ones. One more specifically landed me in jail. But the two brothers, even though they're only brothers by marriage, have never gotten along. I suspect that one got more attention than the other as they grew up, but it's none of my business, so I've never asked. Truth be told, I really don't care.

"So is this new renter going to get in my way?"

He sighs. "Tegan will be helping, in fact."

"Spectacular," I spit. I prefer to work alone, and if this Tegan guy doesn't know anything about construction, I'll end up spending the majority of my time teaching him.

I learned everything about construction in jail. As a community service, they'd have some of us build houses. The ones with good behavior, anyway. And since I kept my business to myself, I was considered one of the convicts who displayed good behavior. Everything I know, I learned from my time working on those houses, from demolition to building to electrical to plumbing. It helped pass the time.

"Oh, I think you'll get along just fine," Derek adds with humor. I'm not his favorite person in the world, so whenever he gets the chance to rattle me, he does.

I glare at him. "Does this Tegan person know anything about renovations?"

He chuckles. "I didn't ask, but Tegan looked ready to take it on. Expressions were priceless."

"The pink bathroom?"

He nods vigorously. "Priceless."

It probably matched my own when I first saw it too. Honestly, I don't know what it was about the seventies that possessed people to buy pink toilets.

"Tegan wants to keep the sink."

I scowl. "The kitchen sink?" He nods. "Why?"

"Likes it, I guess." He shrugs.

What dude likes an old farmhouse sink? And, if given the chance, why would anyone want to keep something old in favor of something new? The option is there. Derek has a shit ton of money, so why would we keep it?

"And you're okay with this?" I ask with disbelief.

He shrugs again. "It adds charm, don't you think?"

I take several gulps of my beer to wash away the ass-chewing I want to give him. "Sure," I say instead.

"Great." He slaps his thigh. "I'll have a dumpster delivered today."

I look at him skeptically. "Think you can get old man Greg to get off his ass and drop it off?"

"I'll go down to his office myself if I have to." I can see the determination set in his eyes. He'll find a way, I'm sure of it.

He heads to the door, and I call at his back, "Anything I need to know about this guy?"

A slimy smirk takes over his shrewd lips. "I'd be careful how you talk to Tegan. Sensitive, that one."

"What's that supposed to mean?"

His smirk widens into a knowing smile. "You'll see."

He opens the door and leaves, whistling all the way to his car. I get up and slam the door shut. *Fuck this bullshit.* This isn't what I signed up for.

CHAPTER 3
TEGAN ADAMS

Tori looks at my open suitcase with disgust. It's sitting on the bed wide open, its contents on full display. She came over for supper and to help me unpack, and now that supper's over…well, she's not happy with me.

I press my pointer finger to my chin, waiting for her to spit out what she's holding back.

"Did you…did you just throw everything in here?" She picks up a wadded shirt and turns a frown in my direction. "You didn't even bother to fold."

Tori isn't shaped like me. Where I'm thicker—curvier, as I like to think of it—she's thin. Her features are more pixie-like: short nose, round eyes, and slender cheekbones, unlike mine, which are more prominent. My jaw is square, and my nose is longer but not too long, with a smattering of freckles across the bridge. We share the same hair and eye color, though: blond with blue eyes. I just keep mine past the shoulders while she cuts hers above the collarbone.

I wince and run a hand through my hair, untangling a knot at the ends. "I was in a hurry."

"More like a mad rush," she grumbles. "Did you miss me that much?"

I laugh a little, take the shirt from her, and chuck it at her playfully. She catches it, matching my grin with one of her own. It reminds me of our playfulness in college, and my heart warms as all the memories surface. "Of course."

We were dormmates at Illinois University, and we both have a pile of student loans to prove it. Tori's education centered around business, while mine focused on medical. I wanted to be a coroner, someone to bring peace to a family by having them know what offed their loved one. It's a morbid occupation, but at the time, I was excited about it.

I ended up getting my degree, not that it did me any good. There were no job openings in the Chicago area, and I had no money to move to somewhere that *did* have an opening. My parents were poor, so I couldn't ask them for the funds either. Plus, the thought of leaving them made my heart hurt. They were both in their early forties when they found out that my mom was carrying me. Their little miracle, they called me. I've tried to live up to that standard my entire life, and when they grew older and needed my help more, it gave me more reason to stay.

But now they're gone, and a part of me died with them. My only family. My only ties to Chicago.

The only place I could get a job after college was the funeral home, and though I was qualified, I was never allowed to prep a body for its final rest. The owner was a prick, and because I was a woman, I wasn't capable, in his eyes, of doing anything but planning and running the funerals.

I look at my best friend as she folds the shirt that I threw at her.

Tori dropped out of college after two years, leaving me all alone. She had thought she learned everything she needed to, and aside from that, she's not one to stick around for long. I never held it against her, and still don't, that she moved on before I could. And she'll never admit it, but the guy she was dating, the guy who almost ruined her life by selling her identity online, nearly broke her. I think she may have quit college and moved to Fairview to run away and lick her wounds.

But apparently, it was the best decision she ever made because she's built quite a life here. Dug her claws in and refused to leave. There's still no man in her life, though. She doesn't trust them enough to keep them around for long, and I can't say I blame her. What that guy did to her almost made me swear them off too.

"You're staring," she singsongs as she sets the folded shirt in a dresser drawer.

"Am not."

"I'm beautiful, I know."

I pick up a pair of wrinkled jeans that came straight from a hot dryer when I threw them in my suitcase. The pant legs whip as I snap them in the air. "Just feeling lucky."

"Lucky, huh? And why is that?"

I bump my shoulder against hers as she moves

back to the suitcase. "That I still have someone to share my life with."

She glances at me before grabbing a pair of socks. "Do you want to talk about it yet?"

"About what?" I ask, even though I know exactly what she's talking about.

"Your parents. Them dying. You know, the shit you have yet to discuss with me."

I sigh. "They died. There's no use talking about it."

She whips back toward me and blindly shoves the socks into the top drawer. "Your parents died a horrific death, Tegan. I mean, at least they were sleeping, but no one should die in a house fire. That had to leave a mark on you, or you wouldn't have rushed to get here like this."

Setting the folded jeans down on the bed, I turn to face her with my arms folded across my chest. "It was horrible, okay? It was. And what came after was even worse, but—"

She nearly snarls when she cuts me off. "Your boss should have never made you be in charge of their funeral. That was so sick and twisted."

It may have been a closed-casket funeral, so I never saw their charred bodies, but it made me sick to my stomach to plan and attend their funeral at the same time. Many tears were shed that day, and I'm surprised I even got the job done. It definitely didn't do anything to help me heal, that's for sure.

I quit my job the next day. I have zero regrets about that. And the day after that, I made my quick arrangements to move here and be with Tori, the only person I have left.

"Yeah, my therapist wasn't happy," I grumble as I look down at my feet.

"From what you'd told me, he sounded like a good therapist to have."

He was. I met him at a funeral a year ago. I don't know what I must have looked like, but it must have been bad because he approached me and gave me his card, telling me to set up an appointment. It took me a week, but I did end up calling him, and he saw me the next day.

I was depressed. My life was death. I was surrounded by death, afraid of death, and was lonely because of death. He guided me through all that and helped me see the bright side of my miserable job, which was no easy feat. Instead of bringing closure to a family like I wanted when I went to school, I only brought about more tears. More sadness. I felt like the grim reaper, even though I wasn't the one killing anyone.

As soon as I left Chicago, I could breathe again. I felt baptized in a new life. I knew then and there that the choice I made was the right one, even if Dr. Lynn didn't think so.

"Yeah, but he didn't want me to leave," I amend. "And our sessions keep running through my head."

She crosses the short distance between us and places both hands on my shoulders, forcing me to look up at her. "I can tell, just by looking at you, that you made the right choice."

"Oh, I know I did."

"Good." She pecks my cheek. "I just didn't want you to doubt yourself about this."

I shake my head. "I don't. Not one bit. I mean, I wish I had more time to have found a better place to rent because…" I circle my hand, gesturing to the entire house. Tori was appalled when I gave her the tour, so I know she'll know what I mean.

She chuckles and drops her arms back to her sides, returning to the suitcase for another garment. "This will be fun, and you know it. Building something from nothing draws a complete parallel to your life right now. It'll be good for you."

"You're probably right."

She flicks her gaze at me with a knowing look. "You know I'm right."

I bump my shoulder against hers again and suppress a smile. "Thirsty?"

"Got something stronger than water?" she asks with a wiggle of her eyebrows.

My laugh is conspiratorial. "I went to the store this morning. Rum was the first thing I bought." In college, that was our choice of drink. I hadn't forgotten.

"I'll take that then." She nods and continues to sort through my suitcase.

"You got it."

Feeling happier than I have in a long time, I head out of the room, down the hall, and through the still-cobwebby living room. I start to hum to myself as I enter the kitchen, but I stop short when I step through the threshold.

"What the…?"

Just inches from my toes is a rose petal. Just one, beautifully curved by nature, rose-red petal. I bend to pick it up, take a sniff, and then glance around to see if there are more. There aren't, so I head to the trashcan and toss it away. I must have dragged it in somehow when I was putting away groceries.

When I get back to the room with both drinks in hand, I pass her one, and she gratefully takes a sip. "We aren't getting wasted," I warn her when she sips from it again.

"Oh no." She holds up her cup. "It's just been a long day of showing houses to a needy couple with a mile-long 'want' list that you certainly won't find here. One drink should do the trick."

"Just be lucky that I didn't ask to see houses."

She chuckles and sets her drink on top of the dresser. "You wouldn't have been so picky. I mean, look at what you chose. At least, the outside will be pretty once it's mowed."

"Speaking of outside, let's get some air." Even though I cleaned the bedroom and bathroom today, it's still a dusty atmosphere, and I've been on the verge of sneezing for a while now.

She sets the shirt down, nods, and grabs her drink as we head out of the house and into the backyard. The grass comes up to our knees, but the cooler night air brings about a certain comfort. Somewhere in the distance, I can hear the sound of a horse neighing, a reminder that we aren't alone out here.

I met their owner today, a nice elderly lady. Well, I didn't *meet* her. We just waved at each other as she fed them corn husks through the barbed fence.

The night sky is clear, and from where we stand, there are so many stars. These stars were never visible in Chicago, and I find myself marveling at them.

"There are so many," I murmur.

"It's pretty, isn't it?" Tori whispers.

"Yeah," I agree. "I can see why you love it here so much. Everything is so…raw. Untouched."

She nods in answer. "I knew you'd love it too."

I bring the cup to my lips and let the liquid slide down my throat. My eyes pin on the roses that are visible by shadow only, thanks to the moon. "So, what do you know about Derek Wordon anyway?"

She blows out a breath that tickles her hair against her cheek. "He's rich."

"Oh?"

She nods. "He has a lot of business ventures. Occasionally, we rub elbows when he's looking to purchase another house to turn into a rental. He never takes out a loan, either. He just pays with a check."

"Wow, must be nice to have so much money."

She drinks some rum. "He may be a weird-looking dude, but he's successful."

"Is he married?"

She shakes her head. "No kids either."

"Interesting."

"I'm not surprised. He seems to enjoy the bachelor life too much, making his own decisions without having to discuss it with a partner."

I chuckle.

"What?" she asks, looking at me.

"Sounds like you," I admit before taking a sip.

She raises her eyebrows for a moment and then shrugs. "We all have our quirks. So, what's in all that stuff?" She points to the shed and the barn.

"The shed is just full of construction stuff, so I'm

guessing Cole, or whatever his name is, keeps his equipment in there for easy access. The barn has nothing. It's completely empty."

"Probably because a sneeze would tip it over," she says dryly. "He should really just burn it down."

"Yeah, you're right, he should."

"Have you met Cole yet?"

I shake my head. "I don't even know when he's going to show up. What about you? Have you met him?"

She shakes her head. "I know as much about him as you do."

I nod and return to looking at the roses. She follows my gaze. "Derek's stepmother used to grow roses. I'm guessing that's a nod to her."

"I thought he was bitter about the remarriage?" I ask with a frown.

She shrugs. "Men are weird."

"Indeed."

We're quiet for a moment, soaking up the night, and then she reaches over and gently pinches my arm. "Come on. Let's finish the unpacking."

CHAPTER 4
COLE GARNER

Standing in front of the shed, I stare at the back of the house as I get my toolbelt on. There's a girly blue Ford Focus out front that I didn't miss and dutifully blocked in, so I'm mentally preparing myself for some preppy man who wouldn't have lasted a day in prison. No one in this area drives a car like that. Too many rough roads.

Based on the car alone, this already doesn't bode well for me, but at least I'll get some satisfaction out of pushing around a city guy.

The tool belt was exactly where I left it, which was a good start to my morning. I was sure that this dude would have fucked with my shit, trying to get started without me. But everything is the way I left it since I was last here, so I have no reason to complain. *Yet*.

Next, I grab the hammer and head inside, bouncing it around in my palm as I wade through the grass. At some point, I have to tackle this jungle, and I had planned to sooner rather than later, but now that someone is living here, making the house more livable becomes the priority. Even though I'd rather no one live here, I'm not a complete ass.

As soon as I'm inside the dining room, I stop moving and tilt my head to listen. Somewhere in the house, I hear a dresser drawer shut. *A late riser.*

I shake my head, gearing myself up for what a disaster this is going to be, as I head to the living room. Just as Derek promised, the dumpster arrived yesterday. I can see its silhouette through the dirty living room window, and since he said I could throw away anything I found, I'm going to start with the shit on the walls. The counters won't arrive for a while, so I have every intention of taking down this flowery wallpaper in the meantime.

Setting the hammer down on the back of the couch, I gather the old pictures in my arms, head to the door, and use my elbow to unlatch the screen door. The pictures shatter inside the dumpster, and I have to admit it's a satisfying sound. Next, I heave the deer off the wall. I grit my teeth as I tug, hoping like hell I don't take part of the wall with it. It finally releases, and I balance it in my arms, but since it's so large, I can't see properly.

As I make my way blindly to the door, I hear a sneeze. "Can you grab the door for me?" I ask gruffly.

Tegan doesn't answer me, but I hear the hinges squeal, so I press on. As soon as I feel the sun on my arms, I toss the deer head into the dumpster. It thumps, not as satisfying as the glass, but it still brings me a little joy. That trophy was ugly as hell.

Placing my hands on my hips, I turn around...and then stop dead in my tracks.

Standing in front of me, holding the door open, is a woman. She's smiling at me, and the smile lights up her blue eyes like the ocean sparkling under an afternoon sun. Her blond hair is tied back, but a few strands are loose, and they blow in the subtle morning breeze. I can smell the scent of her shampoo from where I stand a few feet from her.

"You must be Cole," she says almost too chipperly.

I narrow my eyes and scan her. She's a little thick around the waist, the kind guys like me like. It gives us something to hold on to, especially when we're plowing in from behind.

Her tank top barely keeps in her large tits, and her shorts hug her wide hips, revealing flawless thighs.

"Are you Tegan's girl?" I grunt out. Derek never said anything about two tenants.

She frowns, pulling her delicate eyebrows down and together. "No," she says, drawing out the word. "I'm Tegan."

I stare at her for a moment as her words register with me. Then, I bow my head and tighten my hands on my hips. A chuckle escapes me. "I'm going to kill him." He led me to believe Tegan was a man. Not once did he correct me. He's a dead man if I have anything to say about it.

"Who?"

I look back at her with my head still bent. "Your landlord."

"Why?" she asks, a little unsure. She looks like she wants to run away.

"You're supposed to be a dude," I amend as I push past her and head back inside the house. I don't have time to worry about why admitting that I wanted to kill Derek worried her.

She follows me, and I can hear the stomp in her gait. She clearly didn't like what I said. The screen door screeches when it shuts. "I wasn't aware that I'm missing a dick. Why does it matter?"

I whip back around to face her and study her for a moment. "You look like you couldn't lift a hammer."

Her eyes narrow, and I can practically see steam coming out of her ears. "Is that so?"

"Yes." I cross my arms over my chest, daring her to challenge me.

Her gaze flicks to the hammer on the back of the couch. When she reaches for it, her arm brushes against my skin. I'd be lying if I said my cock didn't twitch. Even during the brief contact, I could tell her skin was as soft as it looked.

She picks up the hammer and weighs it in her hand. "Satisfied?"

I cross my arms over my chest. "Hardly."

Bringing the hammer up to her face, she presses the head to the tip of her chin as if in thought as she scans my body. Her eyes stop at my crotch. "I could always smash it against your balls as an example."

"You shouldn't even be living here," I say gruffly. Though I want to cover my junk to protect it from her threat, I won't give her the satisfaction. I know nothing about this girl. For all I know, she could be wild.

She raises her eyebrows and tosses the hammer onto the couch. It bounces on the cushion a bit before she says, "Then I suppose it's a good thing you're not my landlord."

I rub a hand down my face. "Do you even know how to do any home renovations?"

"I can paint," she says defensively. "And I'm a quick study."

Sighing, I drop my hand back to my side and survey the room and all that has to be done to just the living room alone. "Teaching someone wasn't what I signed up for."

"Well, an ex-con handyman wasn't what I signed up for either."

I whip my head back to face her. "What did Derek tell you?"

Dare I say it, it's almost cute when she places her hands on her hips, ready to lecture me like an old Italian grandma. "Absolutely nothing, which only serves to piss me off more than the fact that you clearly don't want me here."

I release a slow breath, hoping to gather some patience. I'm glad that Derek didn't tell her anything, though. The town may have known what I'd done, but I don't need her judging the shit out of me. Not that I regret what I did. I'd do it again if given the chance. Maybe I should tell her. If I'm lucky, it just might frighten her off.

Her shoulders slump forward, and her expression softens. "Let's just start over, okay? I'm Tegan; you're Cole. I'm going to help you; you're going to teach me. That's all this has to be."

I grunt in response. I don't see how starting over is going to erase the manner in which we met, but I don't comment on it. "What all did Derek tell you about this property?" I'll need to know what she thinks she's getting into. There's a lot of work ahead of me. *Us.* She needs to be aware of it all.

She shrugs. "Just the basics. The tour, a little house history. Learned a little about his family."

"So, you know this is really his brother's property."

"You mean the missing brother, Neil, or whatever?" I nod. "I thought…"

"His brother is presumed dead, but there are still legal hoops to go through until it can fully become Derek's. Technically, it's not Derek's yet." He may act like it's his, but it's not. Not yet, anyway.

"I thought he was just missing. Like, ran off." She scowls around the place as if Neil himself might show up.

I chuckle at her ignorance. "Have you done no exploring yet?"

She scowls again. "I mean, I've looked around the property, yeah. What else is there?"

I crook a finger at her and take her to the edge of the rug. Keeping my eyes on her, I lift the edge of the rug and feel another bout of satisfaction as she gasps.

"Is that blood?" she whispers. "Holy shit, that's a lot of it."

I drop the rug back down and stand fully upright. When I started, Derek had me pull the rug out of storage to cover it up. He said he didn't want to stare at the reminder.

We're mere inches from each other, enough so that I can feel her body heat. My cock twitches again, but I press on so that she doesn't know just how much she's affecting me. It's been a long-ass time since I've had a woman beneath me.

"The FBI came to investigate once the blood was found, not long after his stepbrother reported him missing. They broke in through the window"—I point to the broken window covered by a plastic trash bag—"just to get inside since the brothers didn't have a key at the time. Found the blood, and not long after, they declared him dead instead of missing. Too much blood."

She raises her wide gaze to mine. "Are you telling me I live in a house where someone died?"

I smirk down at her. "Still want to live here, sweetheart?"

Her thoughts practically run through her flitting expressions, but eventually, she settles on determination. She squares her shoulders. "Yes. I've been around death before. This is nothing new to me."

My smile fades, and I head around the couch, pick up the hammer, and approach a wall. As I pluck a nail from the surface, I say, "Suit yourself."

"I really should have smashed the hammer against your family jewels," she growls at my back.

"Then you'd have to nurse me back to health." I look at her over my shoulder. "Ex-cons don't get great health insurance."

She crosses her arms over her chest, and I turn back to the wall for the next nail. "What were you in for anyway?"

"Does it matter?" I grunt.

"Shoplifting?" I don't answer. "Joyriding?" Again, I don't answer. "Murder?"

I toss the nails onto the floor, grab the hem of my shirt, and lift it over my head. I drop my shirt to the floor and listen with a grin on my face as she falls silent. "Nothing to say now?"

"Why did you take off your shirt?"

"I find that, if you start to get undressed in front of a woman, they stop talking."

I can practically feel her anger directed at my back, and my grin only widens when she spits, "I hope you don't expect me to take *my* shirt off."

I look back at her, catch her staring at my body, and say, "Sweetheart, if anyone is taking your shirt off, it'll be me. And since you don't want to be fucked by a 'murderer,' I suggest you start peeling off the wallpaper." Not that I'd deny her if she asked. Hell yeah, I'd definitely fuck her. If she didn't know that before, she sure as hell does now, judging by her momentarily gaping mouth.

Snapping her mouth shut, her nostrils flare. "Don't you need some sort of solution for that?"

Shrugging, I turn back around to hide my smile. "Don't got any. Better get started. It's going to take a while."

I laugh as she growls, "Asshole."

CHAPTER 5
TEGAN ADAMS

"**W**e can't control someone else's actions," *Dr. Lynn said.*

I rinse my hair out as his advice filters through my head. It's the second day that Cole and I have worked together, but unlike the first day, this day was quiet. I pulled down wallpaper one tiny piece at a time, and he worked on the fireplace. The silence killed me, but I knew if I talked, if I brought up any kind of conversation, it'd end in some sort of banter. So, I worked in silence, and he left in silence.

"All we can do is control our own," he added.

I turn in the shower and scrub the extra conditioner off my face that had flowed down with the water. I honestly don't know how I feel about the handyman. Not once has he given away what landed him in jail. Do I deserve to know? I don't know. I mean, he is in my house. Well, Derek's house, but I like to think of it as my house too. I am paying rent for it, after all. So, yes, I should get to know. He could be a danger to me.

I almost laugh.

The most danger he's presented is fraying my last nerve.

Maybe if I give him a real chance, a third fresh start, things will be different. I can be friends with an ex-con. A surly one. A rude one. I mean, there has to be a reason he is the way he is, and maybe if I remain cheerful and fun, I can help him through whatever haunts him and turned him this way.

I'm determined to make the best of this.

Satisfied with that solution, I shut the shower off and wipe my eyes. I'm just about to whip the curtain back and grab my towel, but I stop. And so does my heart.

Silhouetted through the thin plastic curtain is what can only be a man. A tall one, at that.

Amid the steam of the bathroom, I wait with my hand hovered near the edge of the curtain. My stomach is in my throat, and my breathing is shallow and loud even to my own ears.

"H-hello?" I whisper.

I receive no answer. The figure stands there, and I blink really hard to make sure I'm seeing what I'm seeing.

"Cole?" I try again. He could have returned. Maybe he's a pervert and wanted to see me naked. I mean, he wasn't shy about telling me in a roundabout way that he was sexually attracted to me. Maybe he came back to keep his word.

Somehow, I know that's not true. He would have grunted by now.

I squeeze my eyes shut and gather all the courage I can muster. Quickly, I whip back the curtain and pop open my eyes. If I thought I felt fear before, it's nothing compared to now because nothing, absolutely no one, is standing there.

Tears prick my eyes, and I snatch my towel off the vanity. Wrapping it around my middle, I step out of the tub and wildly search for a weapon of any kind. I still haven't put away my bathroom stuff. They're in a duffel bag against the wall, so I quickly rummage through it and close my fingers around a pair of hair shears. It's not the best weapon in the world, but it's the only thing I have.

Releasing a slow breath, I poke my head out of the bathroom and into the bedroom. No one is there, and everything is as I left it. As I tiptoe to my bedroom door, the floorboards creak in one area, making me stop for a moment to cringe.

"Hello?" I call out with a shaky voice.

I receive no answer.

"Of course not, Tegan," I grumble to myself. "What murderer would answer back?"

Slowly, I creep into the hallway, staying close to the wall as I peek into the other bedroom and then head to the living room. I check all the closets and behind all the furniture, and once I reach the kitchen, I'm about at my wit's end. Confused, I drop my arm that had the shears poised to strike.

I saw someone. I know I did.

I glance at the back door and make a mad dash to it. I fiddle with the knob, but it's locked, and I know I locked the front door. I distinctly remember doing so.

Stumped, I head back to the bathroom to finish getting ready for bed. The shears plop back into my bag, my mind reeling too much to care about what they might have stabbed.

"It could have been anything, Tegan," I tell myself as I brush my hair in the mirror. "Anything at all. Light tricks, even. And—" I scream at the top of my lungs when my phone starts ringing on the vanity.

Hand over my heart, I put down the comb and brace my other hand on the vanity to keep me steady. My entire body is shaking, and I let out a nervous laugh at how ridiculous I'm being. The fact that I'm alone in the middle of nowhere is playing tricks on my mind. Making me see things that aren't there. That's all this is.

My breath whooshes out of my flared nostrils as I release it before I pick up the phone. Tori's face comes into view as soon as I accept the incoming video call.

"Hey beau—" She frowns. "Are you laughing? I hope it's not at me."

I laugh again, both out of lingering nervousness and out of new humor. It was the exact distraction I needed because she looks utterly horrid. "What's all over your face?"

"A clay mask!" she says defensively. Everything on her face is covered in a layer of brown minus her eyes and mouth. "It's supposed to restore skin."

"Sure," I say. "And the curlers?"

She touches them gently. "Trying something new I saw on a video."

"Right," I chuckle. I pick up my comb and drop it back into my bag. I should unpack this stuff, but honestly, if I put it away in the drawers, I'll just have to move it all again when we rip this horrendous vanity out. I really see no point.

"How was your day?" I ask as I set the phone back on the vanity and pull out my bottle of lotion. It's scented like mangos that an ex-boyfriend said complemented the smell of my skin. I took that to heart, and even though we broke up, I still believe him. It's not a bad smell. I actually prefer an almond scent, but once you get complimented about something, you tend to keep doing just that.

She sighs. "It was a long-ass day at the shop that ended with a last-minute house showing in Spring City."

I put my face into view of the camera. "Did you get a sale?"

She shakes her head. "Not yet. They're doing the counteroffer back-and-forth crap. My phone keeps dinging with their messages. I hope they know I'm going to bed soon. I have a long day of going through boxes tomorrow."

"How's setting up the shop going anyway?"

"Well, it'll be a lot better once I get you in there. Tomorrow, right? For such a small shop, you wouldn't believe how many boxes there are."

I smile at her and then begin to apply eye cream. I may not have wrinkles yet, but I'm trying to be proactive. The number of wrinkles my mother had was alarming, and since I take after my mother…it's just better to start early.

"Definitely. I'll get donuts and coffee." After Cole and I were done working today, I went into town and explored a little. There wasn't much to explore, just a few shops, but they did have a tiny café downtown that doubles as a bakery. I stopped in to see what they offered. Of course, as soon as I entered, the smell of blueberry scones and coffee hit me. I bought both. How could I not?

They were as delicious as they smelled, which could be dangerous for me. Not only will I have trouble keeping what little figure I have, but my wallet will cry. I didn't come here with a ton of savings, just the money I got from selling my parents' charred plot to their neighbor. And though I'm starting a job with Tori, that doesn't mean it'll pay well. In fact, we hadn't discussed payment. I didn't really care at the time. I'm sure she won't screw me over, but I know she can't pay much. The shop hasn't made her any money yet since it's not open. Everything in that shop was paid for straight out of her pocket. She may make good money from being a realtor, but that doesn't mean she has a whole lot to pour into the business.

Ergo, I need to be frugal.

"Oh, get me that berry cream one."

"The white frosting?" It had been an option before I decided on the blueberry scone.

She nods as I screw the lid back onto the eye cream and drop it into the bag. I pick up the phone and say, "You got it."

"You seem like you're in a better mood than yesterday."

"I blame the blueberry scones," I say with a laugh as I zip up my bathroom bag.

"They are delicious," she agrees, chuckling with me. "How did today go with Cole?"

I stand fully upright, blow out a breath, and shrug. "He didn't say a word to me. We worked in total silence."

Her eyebrows raise, which is almost too hard to see because of the dried clay on her face. "So you didn't find out why he went to prison?"

"Nope."

"I mean, I could ask around, but…"

I shake my head. "No, don't do that. It would just feel wrong to find out that way."

"Okay," she says with a tiny lift of her shoulder. "Let the mystery continue then. A hot mystery man." She grins. "I like the sound of that."

"He is *not* hot."

She laughs at my lie. "Don't even try it, girl. He's a panty dropper."

I nibble my bottom lip and lean against the damp wall. Okay, so maybe he is attractive: short-cropped dark hair, perfect square features, and his full, kissable lips. And *my god*, his body. That first day, when he took off his shirt…*muscles for days*. Muscles that rippled with each tiny movement. And I only saw his back, too.

A wide grin shows all of her straight, perfect teeth. "You're thinking about him naked, aren't you?"

I scowl. "Am not."

45

"I have, and I've only seen him in passing. I'm sure every woman has."

I roll my eyes. "Not gonna happen, Tori."

She sits up straighter, and it's then that I get the view of her oak headboard. "I heard he has a ripped body."

I glance away and bite my bottom lip.

"Oh god! You've seen it, haven't you?" Her tone is high-pitched, demanding answers.

"I might have," I say while studying the wall by the mirror.

She squeals. "Details!"

My shoulders lift and fall in a small shrug. "He's just really ripped." I look back at her with narrowed eyes. "He probably gained all that muscle from prison."

She waves a hand in front of the camera. "Who the hell cares where he got them? Could you imagine what it'd be like having sex with all that muscle?"

I pinch the bridge of my nose and grumble under my breath for a second. "I try not to imagine such things."

"Only because it'll make you all hot and bothered. You should try to lay on some moves."

Dropping my hand back to my side, I say, "He's not my type, Tori."

A disgusted noise comes from the back of her throat. "I've seen your type. It's pathetic."

I frown. "My choices in men are not pathetic."

"They're safe, Tegan. Boring. So yes, a little pathetic. I thought you came out here to live a little? What better way to do it than with Cole?"

"You mean an ex-con?"

"It's better than the beekeeper you dated. Or the charity owner. Or the pet rescuer."

"All sensible men who did *not* go to prison for God knows what."

She moves the phone closer to her face. "Just think of the thrill, Tegan."

"Why don't you fuck him then?" I ask, exasperated.

She shrugs a little. "He seems like the type that would take a lot just to get to your front door. But you already have him in your house. When was the last time you got laid?"

A long, long time ago. "Does it matter?"

"As your best friend, yes, it matters." She moves so that she's lying down on her bed. "You know what? You just gave me a mission."

"Oh god," I mumble.

"I'm going to get you laid."

Knowing I can't stop her now because, once she has an idea, she sticks with it, I say, "Sure, Tor. You do that."

She says something in response, but I don't listen. All I hear is the floorboards creaking in my bedroom. Without a second thought, I glance into my bedroom, solely distracted by Tori's mission.

It's an old house. Things are going to creak. But what stops me is the rose petal now on my pillowcase.

"Tegan?" Tori calls. "Are you listening?"

"Hmm?" I ask as I head into my bedroom. I pick up the rose petal with a frown. "Not really."

"What are you looking at? Your eyebrows are all scrunched up."

I cock my head to the side and then glance around my bedroom. "A rose petal."

"Where the hell did that come from?"

Rubbing the petal between my fingers, I say, "I have no idea, but tonight is full of strange things."

"What do you mean?" she asks with genuine curiosity.

I go on to explain the whole man behind the curtain thing, and all she does is cluck her tongue. "Maybe you have a ghost. I mean, you did tell me yesterday about Derek's brother. What was his name again?"

"Neil." I glance at his picture still hanging by the cheval mirror. I hadn't taken it down. For some odd reason, it felt wrong to, like I was disrespecting the dead.

"That's right. I remember when that was huge news, but at the time, I didn't pay much attention to it. Maybe he is actually dead." A wicked smile makes her cheeks puff out. "Maybe he's haunting you."

"Ghosts aren't real," I say as I lower my gaze and look in the cheval mirror. From where I stand, only half of me is reflected in it. The other half shows the pasture out back, visible through the nearby bedroom window. But even my own voice doesn't sound convincing. "I should go. Tomorrow is a big day."

"Right!" she exclaims. "Remember the berry cream donut. White frosting!"

I nod and disconnect, but I can't help but stare at half of my reflection. I came here to escape death.

Death has followed me. Could it really be a ghost? Or was someone truly in my house?

I'm not sure I want the answer to either of those questions.

"Death is a natural phase of life, Tegan," Dr. Lynn always said. "Learn to live with that fact and you'll have a much more fulfilling life."

CHAPTER 6
COLE GARNER

I turn my truck into the cemetery. I wasn't going to come, but I went home for the night and couldn't stop thinking about her. *My sister.* She'd been on my mind all day, our memories whispering in my ear while I worked with Tegan. She would have wanted me to be nice to her. She would have wanted me to give the girl a break, and she'd be right. But try as I might, I couldn't come up with anything that would be "nice." Not that there weren't nice things to say, there were plenty, but I couldn't figure out how to word them right.

So I kept silent.

I tried to forget about this day. Working out until I maxed out did nothing to pull my sister from my thoughts. This day, three years ago, I got notified in my jail cell that she was dead.

She was the entire reason I went to prison in the first place, to protect her. I'd do it again, but imagine my heartbreak when I couldn't protect her from death.

She was young. Too young to leave this world. And the way that she went . . .

No one should be so far gone that suicide is the only way out.

They told me that she hung herself in her closet. Closet bars aren't that high up. She could have stood and put an end to her death wish, but she didn't. She had to have bent her knees and hung there until she was gone.

I had beat the shit out of my cellmate that night. Even after all the details the guard gave me, he asked if my sister had been hot. I saw red. My fists went flying, and guards had crowded into our cell to pull us apart. I was put in solitary confinement for a month because of it too. Him? He didn't even get a slap on the wrist.

She was, though, always had been. She was stunning, and because of her doll-like looks with wide brown eyes and pale skin with rosy cheeks, she'd been taken advantage of at an early age.

The cemetery is pitch black, but the bright moon makes the tombstones cast big shadows. Unlike Derek's rental, the cemetery is surrounded by great openness. Hills and wildflowers, and beyond is a small mountain that I can barely make out. It's a nice final resting place, one I hope to eventually be buried in when my day comes. Right next to my sister, where I belong.

I pull up to her row and shut the truck off. My fingers grip the steering wheel so tightly that the worn leather squeaks. I've only been here once before. It was the first place I stopped when I was released because some part of me didn't believe it to be true. But as soon as I saw her name on the stone…I knew. It was certain. She was buried six feet underground, and there wasn't a damn thing I could do about it.

Looking beside me, I stare at my leather wallet for a moment before picking it up. I carefully open the flap and dig into a hidden pocket. It had taken a while, but I had convinced the funeral home to print me an obituary. I cut out her picture and stuck it in my wallet, and in moments of weakness, I pull it out. I do so now, careful not to bend the edges.

The moon provides enough light in my truck to see my sister's smiling face. It's her school portrait, and she's a lot older in this picture than when I was arrested. She had lost her baby cheeks, and her lips went from a pink to a rosy red. Her brown hair is less ratty than when she was a ten-year-old, her age when I was taken away. It was more smooth and silky. Even the camera captured that.

Her smile, however, doesn't reach her eyes. It hasn't since before she was ten, but she looks so dead inside. It makes me wonder if my leaving her did this to her or if it was what happened to her in the first place.

I run my thumb over her face. We have similar looks. Not all foster kids who are related know what their parents look like, so I have no idea who we take after. I was old enough to remember when we were placed in the foster system, her as a baby and me at age seven, but I couldn't picture my parents' faces to save my life. I have no memories of them. I just remember the badges coming and taking us away.

Sighing, I carefully slide the picture into my wallet and set it back onto the passenger seat. I step out of the car, and a chorus of crickets greets me. For a few seconds, I tip my head toward the sky, inhale a deep, calming breath, and then put one foot in front of the other along the soft, short grass.

I read the headstones as I go along, old family names that have been here since Fairview was founded in 1859. There is only one reason I remember the founding date: our foster parents kept some literature, so if I wanted to read anything to my sister, I had to choose from their history books. One was about Fairview, and that date had always stuck with me.

When I reach her headstone, I stop and stuff my hands into my pockets. There are no flowers or wreaths here like some of the other graves have. I never bring her anything. She's dead; she wouldn't know if I did. No, I come here for me. When things get so confusing, I need a little reminder, a little perspective that even a ten-year-old could give me in my teens.

Memories surface. All the times that I had to feed her because our foster parents were "too busy" to feed anyone else but themselves. The bullies I used to chase away when we were in grade school, and I'd pick her up before heading home. One time, those little bastards had cornered her against the side of the school building. All it took was me thundering in their direction, and they scattered like dust in the wind.

The doll I stole from the secondhand store is another fond memory. I got a belt to my ass for that, but our fosters didn't take the doll from her, so I still call it a win. She played with that thing until I...until I was taken away. I have no idea what happened to it.

I have no idea what happened to *her,* either. When I was arrested, that was the last time I saw her. I never got any letters, any visits. I don't know if her new foster family wouldn't allow it or if she somehow blamed me. It could be both for all I know. I'll never get the chance to ask her.

Car lights dance over the graves, and I turn to see who decided to come so late to visit a corpse. I only came this late because she was on my mind. Not many people come after midnight. Or maybe they do?

I shield my eyes when the lights flash directly into them and then grunt when I see the "Sheriff" sticker on the side. "Fucking great," I grumble as I turn back to my sister's stone. I kiss my palm, press it against the stone, and turn to leave. I have no intention of having any sort of interaction with Sheriff George Smith.

My luck runs out, though, because Smith climbs his fat little body out of his car, rounds my truck, and leans against the side of the bed a mere foot from the driver's door.

"Smith," I grunt when I'm near enough.

"What are you doing out here, Garner?" he asks, crossing his arms over his chubby pecs. The uniform does nothing to hide his figure or his love of donuts. The giant bald spot on his head is hidden by a black police hat with a short bill that *normal* cops wouldn't wear, but he just can't help but display his status as sheriff. His feet are small, and his hands are small, but those are the only small parts about him. Unless I count his dick, which I'm sure is the size of a baby carrot. *Poor Mrs. Smith.*

His dull blue eyes pierce mine when I glare at him. "Visiting my sister."

"So late?"

"What else would I do in a cemetery?"

He is silent for a few moments, his eyes narrowing and unnarrowing as he chooses his words carefully. "There's been reports of vandalism from the graveyard manager. That wouldn't be you, would it?"

I place my hand on my door handle and pause there. I knew this conversation wouldn't be pleasant. It doesn't take a genius to know that it's clear that I don't like him, and he doesn't like me, and we both have our good reasons for it. "Do I look like the type that would get my rocks off by throwing around toilet paper over tombstones?"

He shifts so he's angled more in my direction. "It was spray paint, actually. An upgrade from the usual vandalism."

I grind my jaw. "Try the teenagers. They have nothing better to do in this sleepy town."

The nonchalant way that he shrugs one shoulder pisses me off. "You're the only one with a record in town."

"And not one of my charges was for vandalism."

He chuffs. "Are you going to try to convince me that you've been a model citizen since you've been released? Need I remind you of your parole? One call and I can fuck it all up for you."

I grind my jaw because I know he's capable of

doing just that. Itching, in fact. "I haven't done anything wrong."

"Oh, I'm sure I could dig up something," he says with a slimy smile that reveals crooked teeth.

I let go of my handle and step threateningly in his direction. I'll give Smith props, he doesn't cower. "Try it, and that badge won't be able to save you, Smith."

"Are you threatening a cop?"

"Are you threatening to lie to get me put away? Because I have no plans on going back. The only reason I would would be for a damn good reason. Are you going to be my damn good reason, Smith?"

His arms tighten around his chest. "I could put you away for the night just for talking to me like that."

I smirk. "But then you'd have to explain why you've been following me around. Some people would call that stalking. I'm sure whatever lawyer you'd appoint would have a field day with that, especially with our past."

I'm not an idiot. I see him everywhere I go, so I can only conclude that he's been following me, waiting for me to fuck up. But he won't find that here, not in me. I keep to myself, and I only go out when I have to. I'm a model citizen in my parole officer's eyes. Over my dead fucking body is some sheriff with a grudge going to ruin that for me. Not when I just got back up on my feet.

Derek said that Smith wasn't happy when he heard I was being released. He said that the sheriff fought to keep me behind bars. Thankfully, the warden of the prison felt otherwise. He knew why I was there, and he knew that reason was related to Smith. I think some part of him didn't blame me for what I did, and he wanted to shove it up Smith's ass.

"I'll catch you, Cole," he hisses. Spittle flies from his mouth. "At some point, you will fuck up, and I'll be there to put you back behind bars where you belong."

"Then you're going to be waiting a long-ass time for that," I murmur, putting my hand back on the handle again. I wrench the door open and climb into my truck.

He stops me from shutting the door with a snatched-out hand. "This isn't over. It'll never be over."

I twist my lips for a moment and shrug. "I'd do it again, you know."

"What?"

"What I did. The reason I'm an ex-convict. I'd do it again in a heartbeat."

Even in the darkness, I can see his face turn a bright red. "There's a special place in hell for you."

"Probably. I don't fear it." I turn a raised eyebrow at him. "Do you?"

He makes a disgusted noise behind his throat, and I know he catches my meaning. There's no way in hell Smith is going to be with the Big Man upstairs. The bastard turned a blind eye to the reports I'd given about my foster parents, all because they were related. He deserves flames and brimstone, just like me.

"That's what I thought," I growl as I shut my door in his face. I turn the key, and the engine roars to life, the lights illuminating the gravel path in front of me. I salute the pissed-off man just outside of my truck and put my foot on the gas, hoping like hell I run over his damn foot.

CHAPTER 7
TEGAN ADAMS

At this time of morning, the small café is busy. With all the cars outside, some idling and some parked, I know there's going to be a line. I just hope that the numerous customers don't make me late. When I woke up this morning, I told Tori I'd be at the shop in an hour. Half an hour had already passed by while I got ready, and I ran out the door right when Cole walked in.

Thankfully, he didn't ask where I was going. He just gave me a questioning look as I rushed past him and told him I was late. If he had struck up a conversation, I would have hung around to make good on this trying-to-be-friendly thing, and I'd be even later.

I park the car and stare up at the building for a second. It's part of the old downtown strip, and unlike the other businesses, a faded purple awning stretches across the sidewalk, making this place unique. Surprisingly, the purple, although faded, complements the patched brick exterior.

Great windows take up wall space, which would give a view of the inside if the sun wasn't reflecting on them. A few tiny, pink metal tables with equally as small matching chairs are set up outside on the sidewalk. A couple sits at one, sipping their coffee and chatting quietly to one another. I don't recognize them, but then again, I don't recognize anyone here. I only know three people.

As is the case throughout the rest of the town, I notice large flowerpots with roses planted in them. I had looked at them during my last visit to town, and across each one is a plaque that says, "In honor of the Wordon family." I didn't realize what a big deal the Wordons were to this town until that very moment.

Grabbing my purse, I open the door. I'm slammed with the sweet aroma of baking donuts. That smell alone would lure in a person on the strictest diet. It would be a miracle if they were able to resist.

An older, graying woman exits the café and holds the door open for me as I approach. I smile at her and give my nod of thanks before dipping inside.

Just like the awning, the interior has purple walls. It's more lavender, however, and I can tell that it's far fresher than the awning itself. I find that I like the color, actually. It's warming, just like a homemade baked pastry at first bite.

A pastry sounds really good right now. My empty stomach rumbles at the thought.

Dear God, this place is going to be the cause of my thunder thighs and an even bigger ass.

Tables and booths decorate the area inside, all of them full. A family sits at one of the tables to my right, and the little boy grins at me with his milk mustache before he takes a generous bite of his chocolate chip cookie. I suppose there are worse breakfasts. I can't think of any, but honestly, at that age, I would have begged until I cried for a cookie first thing in the morning.

I take in the other faces that don't pay me any attention. Briefly, I glance at the booth filled with local cops. One is wearing one of those police hats, while the others opted for black ball caps. The one with the police hat catches my gaze, and he gives me a little wave. I nod back and turn to the line in front of me.

Only a few people are standing in the line, one of them a little girl with one thumb in her mouth and a blanket in the other hand while she hovers close to her mom's leg. She looks to be maybe two years old, and I smile down at her. I'm just about to crouch and ask her what her favorite donut is when I get a tap on my shoulder.

"You must be the new lady in town," the person says.

I turn and note that the cop with the police hat is no longer in his booth but standing next to me. "I am," I say. I gather my purse in one arm and hold out my hand. "Tegan Adams."

He shakes my hand in his thick one. "Sheriff Smith," he introduces himself.

"Ah," I say as I let go of his hand. "Derek Wordon's stepbrother."

The smile he shares with me is small, and I try to return it more genuinely than him as he proclaims,

61

"The one and only. Are you all moved into my child-hood home?"

I laugh nervously. "Sort of. I unpacked some last night, but mostly, I've been working on wallpaper." I lean in conspiratorially. "There's a lot of it."

His belly laugh is too loud for this space. "My stepdad built it; my mother decorated it. You'll have to blame her."

"Oh, I'd never blame the dead," I say with a wink. "But it's the first thing on my to-do list to make the handyman happy."

His smile fades as quickly as it comes. "That's right. Cole Garner is fixing it up."

"Yeah." I brush hair out of my face and switch the subject because it would seem, by his tone, that he isn't a fan of Cole's. I'm not sure I am either, but I'd rather not have a conversation about someone I don't even know. I've never lived in small towns, but the gossip in one is legendary, no matter where you live. "So, no one has lived in the house before me?"

I keep thinking about how I saw the silhouette of a man outside my shower curtain, and a thought occurred to me: What if someone lived here between Neil Wordon and myself and had a key to get in? It's more probable than a ghost, as Tori suggested. She even texted me this morning to see if the ghost had scared me off back to Chicago.

He stuffs his hands into his uniform pockets. "Nope, just my brother."

Quietly, I say, "I'm sorry for his passing."

His eyes narrow ever-so-slightly, and I almost

don't catch the hostility in them. "He's not dead. Just missing."

I frown a little. "But I thought by the blood—I mean, the FBI—"

"I don't care what they said. He's not dead until a body is found."

Wow. Denial much? I mean, I went to medical school. I know when a stain like that is too much to survive. Maybe he's just so fond of his brother that he refuses to believe he's no longer among the living. It makes me feel a little sorry for him, so I approach my next words carefully.

"So, if he's not dead, where do you think he went?"

He shrugs. "Up and left is my guess."

My frown deepens. "Just like that? No reason?"

Tipping his chin, he looks at me in a way that suggests I'm a little ignorant of their way of life. "Not everyone is fit for the small-town life, Ms. Adams."

"Sure," I murmur, again feeling pity for him that he believes his brother is still alive.

He cocks his head to the side. "Why do you ask if there has been anyone living in the house?"

I cringe a little. "You're going to make fun of me."

A small smile returns to his face. "Try me."

My nose wrinkles. "I think it's haunted."

His eyebrows shoot up into the bill of his hat, and I instantly regret bringing it up. "Haunted?"

I wave a hand in front of me. "It's nothing. Just some strange things. Petals, figures. It's just weird."

"Petals?"

"Yeah." I clear my throat. "Random rose petals. I probably tracked them in or something."

"Interesting," he murmurs.

"Yeah. So, any advice to get rid of a ghost?" I ask with humor.

He wets his bottom lip and looks me dead in the eye. "Well, Ms. Adams, I'm sure I don't have to tell you that ghosts don't exist." He slides a hand out of his pocket and wraps an arm around my shoulders. "Do you think you may be more prone to these kinds of thoughts because of what happened before you came here?"

"Excuse me?"

"Your parents' death," he clarifies.

I slide out from under his arm. "You checked on me?"

He shrugs and crosses his arms over his chest. "I make it a habit to check out everyone who moves into town. I care about the citizens, you know. Need to know who to keep an eye on."

And I'm the one who's paranoid?

After a moment of shock, I sigh. There's nothing I can do about him researching me. I'm sure he's not the only one, either. I suppose that comes with the territory of moving to a town that doesn't even have a grocery store. "I can assure you that this has nothing to do with my parents passing away."

He taps his chin. "Are you sure? It was recent. When loved ones pass away, we need time to grieve."

"I grieve just fine, thank you."

"Have you thought about seeing someone? In the bigger cities, they have people you can talk to."

"A therapist, you mean?" Not that it's any of his business, but I get the feeling he's nosy. Either that or he actually does care. I can't tell which one. Maybe it's both. Anyway, he nods. "I've done that already."

"You see a shrink?"

I pat his shoulder. "They don't like to be called that. And yes, I did. Not anymore, though. If I feel the need to get one, I'll do so, but thank you for your concern. Really," I add genuinely. "It's touching."

"Any time, Ms. Adams," he says brightly, enjoying the gratitude with a beaming smile that reveals crooked teeth I hadn't noticed before. "I'm just a call away if you need someone to talk to before then. Any time of day or night. For any reason. For any problems that should arise."

He produces a card and passes it to me. I take it, look at it for a moment, and then ask, "Should I expect trouble?"

He raises an eyebrow. "You do know who the handyman is, right?"

I purse my lips. "I'm aware that he was recently in prison, but he seems harmless."

Crossing his arms, he says, "A trained lion is harmless until he's not, Ms. Adams."

"Right," I say, sliding the card into my purse. He probably isn't wrong. "Well, I have your number now. Does this mean I get to call you a friend?"

He chuckles. "Call me whatever you like—sheriff, friend, pal, acquaintance. We're a tight-knit community. I want you to feel welcomed."

"Well, I appreciate it."

He looks over and then nods toward the cashier. "Looks like you're up."

I glance away from him and realize that everyone in front of me is now gone. The cashier who helped me yesterday is standing there, the model of patience. "Right. Well, it was nice chatting with you," I say before I step forward and give her an apologetic look.

"You too, Ms. Adams," Sheriff Smith murmurs.

I peek over my shoulder and see him returning to his table.

"Same thing as yesterday?" the woman asks.

Surprised that she remembers me, I blink a few times. "Yes." I clear my throat. "And then I'd like to add another coffee and that berry cream donut," I add hurriedly with a point at the display case. The clock on the wall says I'm already late. Hopefully, the donut will make up for it.

CHAPTER 8
TEGAN ADAMS

"**I**s that the last of the boxes?" I ask as I stretch my back. There are piles of boxes everywhere in Tori's shop, but we got each box moved to the spot where it'll be unpacked. I'm not sure how, but somehow, it has taken us a few hours just to sort through them, and now my back is absolutely killing me. I haven't done this much bending in a long, long time.

"Besides the ones in my office?" Tori asks as she wipes the sweat from her temples with the sleeve of her paint-splattered T-shirt. She had dressed appropriately for this job. Me? I made the mistake of wearing a light pink, floral sundress. In my defense, I didn't exactly know what we were going to be doing today. I knew we'd be unpacking, but I didn't know if anyone important was going to stop at the shop. My goal had been not to look like a hobo, and now I'm paying for that because my strapless bra is digging into the sides of my boobs.

"There's more in your office?" I ask, exasperated.

She shrugs a little. "Well, yeah. But it's just office supplies, and I can do that on my own time."

My shoulders shrug in gratitude, and I look at the wall before us. The floating, light, stained wooden shelves that will go on them are resting against the wall. "Now what?"

"Now, we go next door."

I frown at her. "Why? What's next door?"

She squints at me. "You can be so unobservant sometimes." She flicks a thumb over her shoulder toward the glass front door. "The hardware store. These shelves didn't come with screws."

She begins backing her way toward the door, and after huffing to get a strand of hair from tickling my face, I follow her. The day is already warming considerably, and as Tori locks up the shop, I breathe in the fresh, clean atmosphere that only the middle of nowhere can bring.

"Are you smelling the air?" Tori asks with a chuckle as we begin striding next door. Just like Fairview, Mount Pleasant has an old downtown strip full of shops and small businesses. I'm finding that I like the old, small-town downtown areas. It's quite charming.

"I don't think I have ever breathed in something so clean."

She turns a bright smile toward me. "It sure beats the smell of the city."

I twist my lips. "You're right. I don't miss the stench of cigarettes, car exhaust, and factory smoke. I can really see why you love it here so much."

"It grows on you, doesn't it?"

I nod as she holds the door open for me. As soon as we enter the hardware store, the smell of paint immediately tickles my senses. I rub my nose, not liking the scent as much as the outdoors. "Do you know where the screws are?" I whisper doubtfully to her as we travel deeper into the store.

"Ye of little faith," she whispers back. She gently grabs my elbow and steers me down an aisle that has rows of small plastic boxes containing screws of all kinds. I internally gape at all the options. I had no idea there were this many kinds of screws available.

"Jesus," I hiss as I pick up one particularly large and heavy one.

Tori ignores me while she searches for the right size, browsing the pullout boxes, picking them up, and putting them back. I wait patiently with my arms loosely crossed over my chest. This could possibly take forever, there are so many damn options.

Movement to my left draws my attention. I glance over, and my eyes go wide. "Shit," I hiss, whipping back around and hoping like hell he didn't see me.

"What?" Tori asks absentmindedly. She pulls out another box and makes a noise in the back of her throat. "These are the ones. Can you hand me a bag?"

"Tori," I hiss while I do as she asks, plucking a thin and small plastic bag from the pile of the others and passing it to her.

"What?" she hisses back, finally glancing over at me.

I tip my head, gesturing behind me, and her eyes

flick in that direction before a wide grin spreads across her face. "That's Cole, right?"

I move to the other side of her, using her like a little shield. "Yes, yes, it is."

Cole hasn't seen me yet, but he's browsing the bigger screws that I checked out when we first arrived in the aisle. A look of concentration is etched between his pinched brows as he searches for the right one.

At this vantage point, hidden behind Tori, I can get a good look at him without feeling incredibly guilty or obvious about it. And, damn, he is freaking hot. I mean, I knew he was hot since the moment I met him, but in this moment, staring unabashed, I can really appreciate it.

Today, he's wearing faded jeans that hug a tight ass. His shirt is an orange graphic T-shirt that he cut the sleeves and most of the sides off, leaving a tiny strip of fabric at the hem to keep the shirt together. The homemade cutoff reveals corded biceps and slivers of his abdomen. I can even see the groove of his hip before it disappears into his jeans.

Every move he makes, a muscle ripples. And his hands? Large, calloused, and scarred. I gulp. I mean, I can easily imagine what those hands would feel like on me, and just by imagination alone, my clit tingles.

"Tegan?" Tori's whispering voice filters through my thoughts. I look at my friend. "Did you hear anything I said?"

"I'm sorry?"

She rolls her eyes. "You were ogling." She shoves my shoulder a little. "Just go talk to him."

"No!" I whisper-yell.

"Oh, come on, Tegan. A fly could see that you're attracted to him."

I shake my head. "Am not."

"You're such a liar," she says with a smile. "I thought you came here to change your life. Remember what I said about living a wilder life?"

"Well, yeah." I wrinkle my nose, not liking the direction of this conversation because I know, in the end, she'll get what she wants as always.

She places a gentle hand on my elbow. "Then do it."

"Now?" I hiss.

She nods. "Yes."

"What am I supposed to say?" I nearly spit. Damn her for making me do this.

Her grin turns wicked. "Ask to see him naked for starters."

"Tori," I say, horrified because she didn't whisper it. I don't know if he heard her, but Cole glances in our direction. His gaze lingers on me for a moment, but all he gives is a small, curt nod of acknowledgment. "I don't want to see him naked," I lie, because I pretty much just pictured him naked, and my imagination did not disappoint.

She shrugs. "Sure you do. *I do*. Do me a favor: when you get him naked, snap a picture for me."

"Oh my god," I whisper, placing a hand over my mouth. "What the hell is wrong with you?"

She peeks over at Cole. "Look, if you don't go talk to him soon, he's going to leave."

"But we haven't said two words to each other since we first met. What the hell am I supposed to say?"

She shrugs. "I don't know. Ask him out or something."

"Jesus," I moan quietly, shifting my weight from one foot to the other and then back again. I've never asked a guy out. I don't even know how to approach something like that. They've always approached me and done the asking. "And where would I ask him out to?"

She returns to putting screws in the bag. "There's a bowling alley. Ask him to go bowling sometime."

"Bowling?" I ask in disbelief.

"Yes," she says, nodding. "It's a safe option, especially if you're not sure about him because of…well, you know. His past."

I nibble my bottom lip as I look back at Cole. He's busy perusing the big screws again. Could it really be that easy? He hasn't seemed interested in any conversation since our spat, so what if he detests the idea of hanging out with me?

Wrapping an arm behind me, she pushes me in his direction. "Go."

I shoo her hand away and put one tentative step in front of the other before squaring my shoulders and striding in his direction. I can do this. I want to be on friendly terms with him at the very least. Tori's right. Bowling is the safe option, and who knows, it could be the start of something bigger.

I mean, I can deny my attraction to him to Tori all day long, but deep down, he makes things tingle in me both physically and emotionally—even when we argued—and especially here where he looks completely relaxed. There's just something sexy about a hardworking, hardheaded man in a relaxed environment. I hadn't been aware that it was something that would give me goose bumps and stomach butterflies until this very moment. Or maybe the butterflies are from me being absolutely terrified about approaching him. Rejection can sting, I hear. And going by our other interactions, this could end horribly.

"Hi, Cole," I squeak when I'm beside him.

He turns pinched brows in my direction, and when he realizes it's just me, the space between his eyebrows smoothes. I'm completely aware when, just for a second, his eyes skate down my body. "Hey," he grunts.

I fidget a little. "Getting things for the house?"

He nods, grabs a screw, and checks the size.

"You sure are working hard," I ramble on because clearly this is going to be a one-sided conversation. My hopes dash, making the words just spew out of my mouth. This was a bad idea. "I really do appreciate it. And I'm sorry I had to rush out this morning. I started working next door, and I was already running late when you walked in."

A grunt is his only response. Damn, he doesn't make this easy, and if it wasn't for the moment when he checked me out, I would just walk away and deem him uninterested.

I glance back at Tori, and she gives me an encouraging wave. Releasing a slow breath, heart thundering, I turn back to Cole. "So, I have a question."

The way he looks at me from under his lashes

makes my nipples pebble. Damn traitorous body. It's completely sexy, especially since his lashes are long and dark. I can imagine him looking at me like that while his face is buried between my legs.

I swallow hard as he asks, "And what is that?"

Clearing my throat, I blurt out, "Do you want to go bowling sometime?"

Both of his eyebrows raise, and my heart sinks because I can *feel* the rejection coming.

When he says nothing, I stutter on. "I-I mean, not t-today. Like, maybe someday. When we both have f-free time."

A small smirk tips his lips up. He knows that he makes me nervous. I can tell by that one look. What I can't tell is whether he *enjoys* that he makes me nervous. "I'll think about it."

Nodding vigorously, I take a step in Tori's direction. "Well, you know where I live. Ball is in, um, well, you know. Your court."

His smirk grows a little as I quickly back my way toward my best friend. He watches me the entire time with a look of amusement. As soon as I turn my back to him and face Tori, I can feel my face heat with embarrassment. I could have handled that way better. I was a damn stuttering fool because, not only is he incredibly attractive, but I can't forget that he's an ex-convict for reasons that I do not know. He's intimidating in every way.

Tori claps her hands quietly, the bag full of screws jostling in the crook of her arm. "Look at you, living wildly. How'd it go?"

"Um—" I look back over my shoulder and find that Cole is gone. "He said he'd think about it."

"Well, that wasn't a no."

"Yeah," I respond, blowing out a breath and turning back toward Tori.

"You sound super disappointed," she says as we begin strolling down the aisle in search of the cash register.

Am I? I mean…okay, yeah. I'm disappointed. "For the obvious reasons."

She hooks her arm through mine. "Remember when I told you he'd be the kind of guy that's hard to get to your doorstep?" I nod. "Give it time. You'll see him every day. He'll warm up to you, and then you can ask again."

I chew on the inside of my lip as we reach the cashier. She's right. He didn't say a single word to me yesterday, and the day before, we argued. We haven't exactly had the best of starts to things, but I do want to get to know him more. He intrigues me, and he's attractive, and I know that, somehow, I'll get over the intimidation thing. Maybe.

But seriously, "attractive" is putting it mildly.

Releasing my lip, I just feel more firm about getting on friendly terms with him, at the very least, to make our time together pleasant. I do want to help him too. I can tell that, in some way, he's suffering, and somehow, I might be the remedy.

And also, I'd be lying if I said I didn't want to explore the weird tingling thing I felt today being in his presence. That was definitely new to me, and it deserves further investigation.

With a better feeling about this, I walk back to the shop with Tori, making small talk. All the while, I think of ways that I could possibly make Cole's and my time together tomorrow more pleasant. And then after that, it's up to fate.

CHAPTER 9

COLE GARNER

No matter how many times I enter this house, it still smells dusty and musty as hell. I let the door shut behind me and set the wallpaper stripper just inside the door by my feet. The living room is empty, so I listen for Tegan. Her methodical laugh filters down the hall, followed by undistinguishable chatter. No one else is parked outside this morning, so I can only conclude that she's on the phone.

I get a good look at the living room. I may have worked alone yesterday, but I left the wallpaper alone. It's exactly as Tegan left it. It wasn't because I wanted to be a jerk and not help her get ahead or feel bad for how I treated her about it in the first place. Nor was it about my semi-rejection at the hardware store yesterday. It's because I had more pressing shit to do that I know she couldn't handle alone, like mowing the grass.

I borrowed a riding mower for it and had to make

several passes just to get it all one length. I only tackled the front yard, but it looks better than it had. At some point, I'll have to pull all the overgrowth in the front of the house, but I'll save that for another day.

Wallpaper still covers two walls. If we both work on it today, we can move on to other shit. Hell, she could even start painting.

I hear a bedroom door open. "I have to go, Tori. I think he's here. Okay. I'll talk to you later and tell you all about it."

Tori? I only know one Tori, and she works in real estate. It's not exactly a common name for an area like Fairview. Never worked with her myself, but I see her signs around town on the lawns of houses for sale. I wasn't aware that Tegan knew anyone here, but they're clearly friends if they're talking this early in the morning.

As she rounds the corner, she pulls the phone away from her ear and presses a button on the screen. She lifts her gaze to me, and a smile grows that's better than the sunrise outside.

Unlike the sundress yesterday, today, she's wearing nothing but a gray tank top and a pair of black gym shorts. My cock stiffens at the sight of more bare skin, and I work to keep my eyes on her face instead of having them wander to her tits, which are threatening to spill out the top of her tank top.

The dress she wore yesterday? The top half had molded to her like a second skin. It was hard not to skate my eyes across her to imagine what she looked like underneath.

"Right on time," she says chipperly. More chipperly than I would have thought for someone who was semi-rejected yesterday. Perhaps she didn't see it that way. It's not that the idea didn't appeal to me. It's just that I'm no good for her, and I know it. She may not, or she's choosing to ignore that fact, but I do. "Do you want coffee? I was just about to make some."

I scratch the back of my neck. "Sure."

She nods at me, making to twist and move through the living room, but pauses instead. She looks down at my feet and frowns as she reads the label of what I brought with me. "You brought a stripper?" Her gaze returns to mine, but the frown remains in place. "That was nice of you."

I grunt and lie, "I can be nice."

She narrows her eyes, but it's in a playful sort of way. "That has yet to be determined."

I raise both of my eyebrows, not really sure how to respond. I can't remember the last time someone teased me.

She slaps her hips. "Why don't you get that ready? I'll go get the go-go juice."

"Go-go juice?" I say with a little humor in my tone.

Walking past the couch, she pauses and glances over her shoulder. "Did they not have coffee in prison?"

"Wouldn't you like to know?"

"You're not going to tell me anything, are you?" She huffs like my sister used to when she didn't get her way with me.

I stare at her for a moment, then bend to pick up the stripper. Always so damn curious about my time in prison. Honestly, she could ask around town to see why I was put away, but the fact that she's still completely oblivious tells me that she's respecting my privacy. And the fact that she's trying to be friendly with me tells me she isn't afraid of me like everyone else. I must have underestimated her personality. And dammit, her respect for me only serves to make her more attractive than she already is.

I wonder if she knows what, exactly, her choice of clothing is doing to me. It's been a long time since I've had a woman beneath me, way back when I was still a minor. I haven't slept with anyone since I got out, having to use my hand instead because not many people in town will sleep with someone like me. Not only that, but I'm trying to keep my nose clean. A partner tends to complicate things if you happen to choose the wrong one.

"Guess not," she murmurs.

As she disappears to the kitchen, I take the stripper and set it behind the couch before heading outside to the shed. When I pass through the dining room, I hear the coffee pot brewing in the kitchen while Tegan hums softly to herself. The scent reaches my nose, and I inhale it a little. It's been a while since I've had coffee. I haven't bought a machine yet, haven't truly had a good reason to. But now that I smell it, I make a mental note to do so.

I used to be addicted to the shit in prison, even though it was shitty coffee. Police station coffee is better, but I drank copious amounts of it because what else was I going to do? Watch the birds freely come and go on top of the barbed wire that wrapped around the top of the prison yard's concrete wall?

Aside from lifting weights, drinking coffee was my favorite pastime when we were allowed it for good behavior. They dangled it over our heads like a fucking carrot. A lot of men used it to talk to one another, the men who had been there since they were young adults and were now aged to graying hair and deep wrinkles. Me? I used it to have some time alone. There aren't a lot of places to have alone time when you're behind bars.

I wade through the grass to get to the shed, wrench the rusted door open, and pull out the supplies we'll need. By the time I get back inside, Tegan is in the living room, gripping both mugs of steaming coffee.

She holds them up. "Found these at the second-hand store. Fifty cents each. Even though they're ugly, I couldn't pass up that price."

I twist my lips into an awkward smile and take an offered mug.

"I watered it down a little," she adds with a grimace. "I make mine strong, and I wasn't sure how you liked yours."

I take a sip as I set the supplies down on the couch in silence. What the hell do I say to that? Thank you? It's fine?

As I contemplate how to respond, she says, "You don't talk much, do you?"

"What makes you say that?"

A mocking, shocked look widens her features. "You *do* speak."

"I've spoken," I defend.

She places a hand on her hip, and my eyes immediately go to the action, taking in the curve of her thick waist. It takes everything I have to tear away my eyes. "You've said the bare minimum since our initial fight."

I shrug as I drink more coffee. Since it's watered down, it's not as hot.

Setting the mug on an end table, I grab the sprayer and the stripper and head to the kitchen for the sink. I mix the concentrate and peek over my shoulder. Absent her coffee, Tegan stands there, fidgeting. It makes her tits bounce, and goddamm…

"So, how does this work?"

I turn back around to fill up the sprayer with the mix. "I soak it. We peel it."

"Oh," she says, surprised. "You're helping?"

I nod.

"If I didn't know any better, I'd say you're trying to get on my good side."

I have the urge to pinch the bridge of my nose. She's reading too much into this. Instead of doing just that, I put the sprayer back together and turn to face her. She wears this expectant look like she's demanding for me to respond, but instead of giving her what she wants, I push past her. As I do, her chest rubs against me. I grit my teeth, and as soon as my back is facing her, I adjust my pants because of the growing appendage.

I plug the sprayer in and get to work with Tegan as my watchful eye. After a few minutes, she asks over the noise, "Can I try?"

The sprayer sputters as I pause in pumping it. I look at her consideringly. When I notice that she doesn't seem the least bit shaky about trying something new, I pass it to her.

"Apply more than you think," I murmur.

She starts spraying, but she's standing too far from the wall. Without thinking, I place my hands on her hips and move her forward. It's the wrong move because, now that my hands are on her, I know exactly what she feels like. Soft. Shapely. And this close, I can smell her scent, even over the stinging aroma of the stripper.

Peaches. She smells like fucking peaches.

I bite back a growl of approval as I peel my hands off of her once she is an appropriate distance from the wall. I watch her backside as she does the job. Her ass is perfectly round, and I imagine my handprint outlined across the cheeks.

Her ass is definitely biteable, but as I raise my gaze higher to her hips where they dip to meet her ass, I realize how damn inviting they are. I'd place my hands there as I drove into her over and over again. It's the perfect place to grab on, the perfect place for bruises from me holding on tight.

I raise my gaze higher to the back of her bare shoulders. Her skin is flawless. Creamy and slightly tanned. It makes me wonder, if I bite the crook of her neck from behind, would she moan? Is that a sensitive spot for her? How would her moan sound?

The idea of her moaning makes me adjust my pants again, and just as I finish doing so, she turns around. My gaze immediately goes to her chest, where…son of a bitch, she isn't wearing a bra. Her pebbled nipples poke through her tank top.

Either she doesn't notice me staring, or she doesn't bother commenting on it because she says, "Is that soaked enough?"

Soaked. If this keeps going the way it's going, my briefs are going to be soaked from precum.

"Hmm?"

She frowns. "The wall?"

I look at the wallpaper, focusing back on the task at hand, and give a nod.

Her hair falls over her shoulder when she tips her head to the side. "You okay?"

"Fine," I grit out, focusing on anything but her chest.

"You don't seem fine. You seem...you seem like a caged animal."

"I said that I'm fine."

"Are you sure, because—"

Her words cut off as I snap my gaze to her and stalk toward her. She backs up into the wall that already has the wallpaper torn off, and when her shoulders hit it, she drops the sprayer to the ground with an unsure expression. I invade her space, press my chest to hers, and grip her jaw.

And then I take her mouth.

At first, she freezes, stiffening in my embrace, but when I wrap my other hand around her backside, squeezing my arm between her and the wall, she seemingly melts against me. Her lips start to slide along mine, and I angle her head back to deepen the kiss before sliding my hand down from her jaw to collar her neck.

Unable to help myself, I squeeze a little.

Pulling back, I take in her face while rubbing my thumb over her rapid pulse. There's fear there, but I see the flicker of arousal in the way she breathes and in the part of her lips. But she doesn't stop me, and I'm glad. She looks so damn hot with my hand around her neck that it makes me wonder just how much of me she can take.

I tease her bottom lip with my tongue until she opens. She tastes like coffee and peaches. I dip my tongue inside, tasting her. Devouring her.

She makes a little whimpering sound when I press her tighter against me. My erection grinds against her stomach, and I want nothing more than to shove it in every hole she has.

Instead, I pull back from the kiss. "If I didn't know any better, I'd say you didn't wear a bra *for me*." I shake my head once while I stare into her bright blue, hazy eyes. "You don't want a guy like me."

She starts to say something, but I let her go and take one step back. I don't miss the red mark around her neck and the sick and twisted thrill that it gives me.

"I'm no good for you," I add with difficulty. It isn't a lie. No matter how much my mind and body scream for her, I won't subject her to a life like mine. She deserves better. She deserves more than what an ex-convict can give her. She's brighter than tying herself to an asshole like me, someone incapable of responding to the same kind of affection she'd surely deliver.

Her chest heaves as she considers my words. "Live wildly."

85

"What?"

She shakes her head. "I'm a big girl, Cole." Crossing the foot-width distance, she grabs the hem of my shirt in her fists, a practical plea. "I get to decide what I do with my life."

And then she takes off her tank top. Her tits bounce as they're freed, and she tosses her shirt next to the sprayer.

Fuck. They're fucking beautiful, full, and decorated with dusty pink nipples. Better than I imagined.

I raise my gaze and see the hunger in hers, and it's then I know that there's no way in hell I'm going to fight her on this.

CHAPTER 10
TEGAN ADAMS

I honestly don't know what I'm doing, but I do know one thing. He made the first move, and now I want more. I'm eager for it, in fact. He feels like playing with fire, like running a fingertip over a flame and betting on which pass will burn me.

Thrilling. Lovely. Wild. Dangerous. Even mesmerizing.

All the things I've never had. All things I want a taste of.

His eyes blaze as they take me in. I've never been shy about my weight, and by the hunger in his eyes, I know I have nothing to worry about. It's just telling of how right I've been about the sneaking glances up and down my body. He finds me attractive, and that makes me feel powerful.

I step back in his direction as he flexes and unflexes his hands at his sides. I can tell that he's fighting with himself on this, so I gently take his hand and flatten it on my stomach. He watches our joined hands as I raise his palm, skating it over my skin and raising goose bumps across my flesh. When I reach just under my breast, I release him and drop my hand, giving him a choice. Touch me, or walk away.

I don't have to wait long for his choice to be made.

His palm stretches up, and he cups my right breast. The calluses on his hand are rough, and they feel amazing on my soft body. I make a little moan at the back of my throat when he squeezes, one particularly rough patch of skin rubbing against my pebbled nipple.

The goose bumps intensify, and electric sensations shoot from my breast and straight to my clit. For a moment, I close my eyes to the sensation, but then they fly open when his other arm wraps around my waist. He hoists me up, turns us around, and sets me on the top of the back of the couch.

Surprised, I grip the edge to keep from tipping over, but I don't need to worry because his arm stays around me for a few seconds to make sure that I'm steady. When he's satisfied that I won't tip over the edge, he lets go, shucks his shirt, and tosses it aside. I take a second to gape at his muscles. I've seen his back, but I hadn't had a chance to look at his front, and my god…every single muscle is defined. Firm. Rippling with each subtle movement, even with each breath.

I have never, and I mean never, seen a body like this in person.

I'm a little shocked, actually, that he only has one tattoo. Right over his heart, he has stitches etched across his flawless skin. It's as if he wanted it to seem like someone had cut him open, reached in, touched his heart, and sewed him back up.

Under the stitches is a date. The first number belongs to this month and the second to a few days ago, but I don't get another second to read the year before he's on me again.

He bends and captures a nipple in his mouth. I suck in a sharp breath as his tongue soothes the slight ache his calluses created. With almost an instinctual reaction, I arch my back into his face, giving him better access as he flicks and rolls his tongue across the tight bud. Each movement feels like goddamn heaven, and a moan starts at the back of my throat and works its way out of my parted lips.

His fingers touch just below my knee before they skate up, over, and above. I wait with anticipation as he toys with the hem of my shorts before his fingers dip inside. Everywhere he touches feels like the fire I draw him equivalent to.

My breathing picks up pace as he growls against my breast. He discovered that I'm not wearing any panties. As a reward, he brushes his fingers against the slit of my pussy, and I swear to God, I nearly fly off the back of the couch. Instead, I grip the edge tightly, my thighs coiled for what might come next.

When he pushes a finger inside me, I gasp. It's been months since I've had sex, and even before then, my exes didn't bother touching me like this. It was vanilla. Plain and always planned. A job and an itch to scratch. No one has taken their time with me. Learned me. Explored.

He crooks his finger and gently rubs a spot inside

me that makes my nipples tighten even further and my lower abdomen clench. My hands fly off the couch and to his shoulders, where I grip his muscles tightly.

Just when I think it couldn't get any better, he uses his thumb to apply pressure to my clit. My moan is deep as he starts drawing lazy circles across it, the rough patches of skin scraping against soft, slick flesh.

My clit. My G-spot. My nipple. My god, I'm not going to last very long.

Quivering. My thighs quiver around him, my toes curling as the fire that belongs solely to him builds in my lower abdomen.

"Oh god, please don't stop. *Please*," I beg in a breathy whisper.

He switches to my other breast, and I gasp. It takes a second for me to coil tightly, and I scream as I come around his finger. His mouth captures my scream, but he rides the waves by continuing to circle my clit. And when I'm done and slumping forward, he nips my lower lip.

Fuck, that was intense. I can feel the sweat prick my pores and bead along my lower back.

My eyes are closed in complete and utter bliss, but when I hear the zipper of his jeans lowering, they slowly open again. I want to see every part of him.

He lowers his jeans and underwear at the same time, and when his cock is freed, I gulp.

He is large. So much larger than I've ever had. I raise fearful eyes to his, and instead of wearing the smirk I'd think he'd have, he stares at me with such intensity that my heart skips a beat. No one has looked at me that way before.

Grabbing my wrist, he guides my hand and wraps my fingers around his warm length. My fingers only go three-fourths of the way around him, but that doesn't seem to bother him because he closes his eyes and bends his head forward, shuddering.

I look back to his cock, to my hand, and begin to stroke him. For something so hard, it's incredibly smooth. His abs shift and ripple with each pass of my hand. A shaky breath is released when he parts his lips and looks at me from under his lashes. God, that look. It's so readable, those "fuck me" eyes, and it's hard to believe that they're directed at me.

He lifts a hand and slides it up my arm until his palm and fingers are wrapped around my throat. Just over my pulse, he presses his thumb.

This action should make me afraid, I realize. But I find it completely thrilling. He could kill me. *Easily*. It would take seconds, and I'd never breathe again. For someone who fears death so much, I seem to have a death wish when it comes to him.

He bends forward and roughly takes my mouth as I continue to pump my hand up and down his length. The kiss is hot, demanding, and in a way, rewarding. I respond in kind, just as eager as him to get one more taste. Our tongues push into each other's mouths, but the way he kisses me tells me he's in charge. It only serves to make me wetter, and I tremble with absolute need. I don't know how he's going to fit, but damn it, I want him.

Time seems to slow, but eventually, he quickly wraps his arms around me, lifts me up, and turns me away from him. He sets me on my feet and gently bites a sensitive spot at the back of my neck, almost as if he just can't help himself.

I moan as he slides down my shorts, and when he bends me over the back of the couch, I feel his corded muscles shift against my spine. He collars my throat again and squeezes a little. The blood gets trapped in my face, but it only serves to excite me, to make my nipples tighten to painful little buds that rub against the roughness of the old couch.

My pussy pulses, anticipating what comes next, but when he notches at my entrance, my body shakes, and I suddenly have doubts. I squeak, "What if it doesn't fit?"

"It'll fit," he grunts.

"W-will it hurt?" I'm trembling now, more afraid of his cock than his hand threatening to cut off my air supply.

"Probably," he says, his voice husky. I get the feeling that he gets off on this—the possible pain and the hand on my pulse. I wonder at it for a second, wondering if it has something to do with the reason he barely speaks. It's as though he thinks if he does, he'll give away a piece of himself that he tries so hard to keep tucked away. A dark past, maybe?

No, not maybe. He went to jail. He definitely has a dark past.

I nod and squeeze my eyes shut. As soon as I do, he shoves inside. I'm so wet that it goes in in one smooth motion.

Arching my back, I scream at the pain of my pussy stretching to meet his size. "Fuck," I hear him hiss. His hand tightens just a little more, and the blood rushes to my face, but he loosens his grip before I get anywhere near blacking out.

And then he starts to move. Tears prick my eyes, and I whimper at first, my walls stretching impossibly too wide, but after a few pumps, my whimpers turn into breathy moans. The pain turns into intense pleasure, and I barely notice his other hand digging into my hips to make sure I stay exactly where he wants me.

"So fucking tight, Tegan," he murmurs in a voice so deep that I almost can't make out the words. "Does it still hurt?" he taunts, and I get the feeling he's daring me to deny it.

Deciding to answer anyway, I shake my head against his hand and push back against him, begging for more. His fingers dig into my hips, his short nails biting my curves. It only serves to heighten my impossibly high arousal.

"Speak, sweetheart." I think this is the most he's ever spoken to me without me prompting the conversation or ending it in threatening tones. I like it, the demanding husky tone, the deep gravelly voice that's laced with lust. The need to control every part of me for his own pleasure. Why do I get off on it?

"More," I whisper because, although it was painful in the beginning, I realize that I enjoyed the pain as much as he did delivering it.

He squeezes my neck. "More what?"

"More please," I rasp. "Harder. Fuck me harder."

He doesn't release the hold of his collar as he picks up the pace and pounds into me. The bite of pain, the pressure of pleasure. My lower abdomen blazes as I fight for air. But I trust him. I don't know why, but I just *know* he has no intention of killing me. The thrill of it, the knowledge that he could easily do so, and the sensations send me over the edge.

My voice is raspy when I scream my release.

"Fuck," he hisses again, releasing my neck, grabbing my other hip, and pounding into me so hard that the couch starts to scoot forward. "That's it, sweetheart. All over my cock."

The orgasm seems to last forever. Heat courses through my body like hot flashes as my pussy ripples around his length, coating him with my cum. My scream turns into loud moans, and when he starts groaning curses, I know that he's right there with me.

His pumps slow as he comes, and I can feel his body trembling behind me. And when he's done, he stills completely before gently pulling out.

I look over my shoulder and watch him as he heads to the kitchen while pulling up his jeans. "Don't move," he murmurs. His back is covered in a fine sheen of sweat, and I marvel at it until he disappears around the corner.

Running a hand through my hair, I try to calm my racing heart. Jesus shit, we just fucked. I fucked an ex-con. For all I know, he could be a serial killer.

I hold in a nervous laugh.

Do I regret it? I ask myself, but I can't find a single regret in any inch of my body. I've never been fucked like that, talked to like that, treated like that. I went into this with the expectations of just being friends, but now, I...I close my eyes. I don't know what this is. An itch scratched? Probably. Like Tori said, he doesn't seem the type to commit. Not that I'd want to.

Right?

Goddammit, that's a lie.

I need to pull myself together and give myself a stern reality check.

He returns with a towel in his hand and cleans me up. "I should have worn a condom," he says quietly.

When he's done, I stand up and stretch out my lower back. I don't miss the way his eyes roam my naked body, nor the flash of attraction and appreciation in them. "I'm on the pill."

His eyes flick to mine, and he gives a curt nod before leaning forward and pressing a soft, tender kiss to my lips. When he pulls away, he brushes the back of his knuckles against my neck, where I'm sure there's a giant red mark. After he's done admiring it, he heads to his shirt and slides it on, giving me the cue to put back on my own clothes.

"Thanks for, uh…thanks for that." God, that was awkward, but my emotions are all over the place, and I'm a little confused at them.

"Anytime," he says, and not in a dismissive way. It was said in the way that he means it, that I should approach him the next time I want to get laid. Although I shouldn't, and I make a mental note of that, because, after that mind-blowing encounter, I definitely want to revisit it again. I just worry that it means more to me than I'm letting on.

To distract myself from that thought, I slip my tank top over my breasts, flick my hair out of the way, and say, "So, I'm making friends in town."

"Mmm?" he hums, his back to me as he heads to the back of the couch.

"The sheriff, to be exact."

He stops moving the couch back to its place, and I don't miss the way his shoulders tense.

I sigh. "Yeah, he doesn't seem to like you either. Why is that?"

Turning to look at me, he rests his ass against the back of the couch where he had me bent over and crosses his arms over his chest. "We have our reasons."

"No answers again?" I ask, lifting an eyebrow. And here I thought a little sex might open him up. "Was he the one who...you know"—I wave a hand around my space—"put you in jail?"

He gives one firm nod, like it was difficult for him to admit it. I feel almost a little guilty for ruining the mood.

I pick up the sprayer and twirl the hose, lost in thought. "I just feel sorry for him, you know? Holding hope that he'll see his brother again. They must have been really close."

"They were," he grunts. "Derek and him, not so much."

"Yeah," I say, sighing. I twist my lips to the side as I add, "Is Derek really a businessman or something? He seems to have a lot going on."

He crosses one ankle over the other. "As of right now, they're not fully his. He's just in charge of them. Everything he has right now, he'll inherit. The thrift store, the bowling alley, this house. Most of the rentals he bought on his own from the income of the others."

"Oh, inherited from his parents?"

He shakes his head. "From Neil."

My expression widens. "I'm sure that pissed him off that he had all these other new responsibilities. Why didn't he just pass some of it off to Sheriff Smith? Was there a will or something?"

"No will," he grunts. "He was court-appointed as next of kin when the FBI declared him dead. There are still hoops he and his lawyer are jumping through before they can fully be his. And Derek likes the income; don't let his newfound business ventures fool you. He had nothing before Neil died. As the second oldest child, their parents left him nothing."

"Everything was left to Neil?" I ask, knowing I'm pressing my luck because he's actually holding a conversation with me. Maybe my pussy really was the key? I should feel a little used, but...well, I don't. Something I did softened him up, and I'd be lying if I said it didn't do something for me too.

He nods. "As for Sheriff Smith, he and Derek don't get along."

"At all?"

His shrug is small. "They have tea every afternoon over lunch at Smith's house, but I think they do that for appearances."

"Right. Small-town gossip."

"They're not fooling anyone."

"That's unfortunate. I bet that Sheriff Smith is bitter toward him because he inherited nothing." I frown. "But then again, he seemed to care more about finding his brother than what his brother had owned."

He nods a little. "Like I said, they were close."

My lips tilt down in a sympathetic smile. "So sad. I've dealt a lot with death, and unfortunately, until there's a body, some people don't accept it."

"He'll move on."

I nibble my bottom lip. "Yeah, maybe," I whisper.

After a moment of silence, he nods to the sprayer and pushes off the couch.

"Right," I say, shaking myself and dispelling the thoughts swirling in my head. "Back to work."

CHAPTER 11
TEGAN ADAMS

I wander through the house with quick and hurried steps. For the life of me, I can't figure out what I'm searching for. Deep down, I just know I need to find something. The anxiety of it all is so crippling that I'm breathing hard and shaking uncontrollably.

Things are getting knocked over as I search under beds and through drawers and closets. When I pass through the living room, pictures fall off the wall and shatter on the floor. I pass it all by as if it were normal. As if I expected it.

"Where is it?" I scream as I head into the kitchen.

"Where's what?" a familiar deep voice rumbles.

I whirl and find Cole standing by the kitchen entrance, his arms crossed over his chest. He's wearing nothing but a pair of jeans.

"I don't know!" I shout at him. "But I have to find it."

He comes to me, arms outstretched to embrace me. "Let me help you."

"No!" I say, pushing him away. "It has to be me. I'm the one meant to find it. No one can help me."

I open the fridge and am slammed with a wretched stench. It smells like a dead deer on the side of the road on a scorching summer day. Inside, I find fruit so rotted that it's shriveled. The steak on the second shelf has gray and deep green mold across the entire surface. And a bloated jug of milk is curdled.

Gagging, I cover my nose and shut the fridge. "Where the hell is it?" I growl.

"You need me, Tegan," Cole says. "You want me. I know you do."

I head to the kitchen drawers. "Of course I do, but that's not what's important right now."

"So then tell me you want me. Say the words."

"Cole!" I snap with my hand on a drawer handle. "I can't right now! Can't you see I'm finding something?"

He shakes his head, and then his whole body quivers. It trembles so much that he starts to become invisible, and when the shaking subsides, standing in Cole's place is Dr. Lynn. "You'll never find what you're looking for, Tegan. You should have never left."

"I don't need you," I hiss. I yank open the drawer, and as I do, dozens of knives fly out. A sharp sensation pierces my chest, and I gasp as the pain blossoms into my arms.

My breathing is labored as I look down and find the hilt of a knife sticking out where my heart is.

"You should have never left," Dr. Lynn whispers. I

barely hear him above the blood rushing through my ears, but I turn to look at him anyway. His hand is by his chin, his fingers curled as he clutches something within them. "Safe is what you need."

"No," I say with difficulty as my knees grow weak. I can feel the blood spreading down my stomach. "I'll never go back. This is—this—is my life now."

Somewhere in the house, music begins to play, a sweet, sad melody from a piano. Where is that music coming from?

In a blink, Dr. Lynn is standing before me, his free hand on the hilt of the knife. In one smooth motion, he yanks the knife out of me. I gasp as his eyes go wide. "You are not alone, Tegan." And then he opens his palm. Rose petals lie there. He inhales deeply and blows them in my face as I collapse to the ground.

MY EYES FLY open as I clutch my chest and gasp for air. The sound of blood rushing through my veins makes hearing impossible, but I wildly search my ceiling as I get my wits about me.

The somewhat familiar space of my bedroom focuses, and I calm my heart rate by counting in my head, inhaling the familiar musty scent of the house.

Everything is dark, but outside my bedroom window, I can see the sliver of a moon, giving me something normal to grasp onto.

My breathing begins to calm, and slowly, the blood pumping in my ears lessens. And when it does, the melody that was playing in my dream filters into my room.

"What the fuck?" I say as I gather myself up on my elbows and look around my black room. I stick a finger in my ear and wiggle just to make sure that I'm actually awake and not headed back into the dream where the melody came from.

But the melody persists, building and building until it crashes into the climax of the song.

Fear pierces my chest, just like the knife in my dream. Someone is in my house, and that someone is playing on the piano.

I grab my phone off the floor and fumble with it as I unlock the screen. After a few button clicks, Tori's number is being dialed. I slide it to my ear as I look wildly around my room for some kind of weapon but come up short. I really should have learned from the bathroom encounter.

"Hello?" Tori's groggy voice comes through when she answers.

"Tori," I whisper as quietly as I can. The piano's song builds again, filling the house with deceivingly beautiful sounds.

"Tegan? Do you have any idea what time it is?"

"Shh. Listen. Do you hear that?" I go quiet, but as soon as I say the words, the piano stops. "Shit," I add in a hiss.

"Hear what?"

"The music," I whisper-yell into the phone.

"You weren't playing the radio?" I hear an edge of impatience to her tone.

"No," I nearly shout. Sliding from my bed, I pad my way across my bedroom and to the door. As I do, the floorboards creak in their usual spot, but I pay them no mind as I put my ear to the door.

Nothing. I hear nothing.

"Tegan," she draws out. A rustling sound comes from her end. "What the hell is going on?"

"Someone was playing the piano in the house," I growl.

Silence stretches on the other end until she clears her throat. "Have you gone to check it out yet?"

"No." My heart skips a beat. "Should I?"

"Yes?" she says as a question.

"What if it's a murderer?" I whisper feverishly.

"A murderer? Breaking into your house to play the piano? God, are you that afraid of death that everyone is a murderer?"

I cringe at how that sounds and put my ear back up to the door. Again, I hear nothing.

"Don't be a pussy. Go check it out."

"Easy for you to say. You're safe and cozy in your townhouse."

"Are you going yet?" she asks impatiently.

Growling, I place my hand on the door handle, gather what little courage I have, and slowly open it. "If I die, I will come back to haunt you."

"Noted," she grumbles.

Tiptoeing, I head down the hall, and as soon as I reach the corner of the living room, I pause and take several deep breaths. And then I turn the corner with my stomach in my throat.

I suck in a breath, more afraid now than I was when the music was playing.

"Well?" I hear Tori ask.

"No one's there," I answer as I step farther into the living room. I tiptoe through the rest of the house as she suggests it, peeking around corners, but again, no one's here. I tell her as much.

"I swear to God, you have a ghost problem."

"A ghost that plays the piano?" I ask as my eyes wildly search the house on my way back to my bedroom.

"Hey, I'm not God. I don't make the rules."

I curse as I enter my room and slam the door. Breathing out a breath, I lean my back against the door and work like hell to convince the adrenaline to leave my body. I have no idea how I'm going to go back to sleep like this.

Pinching the bridge of my nose, I admit, "I can't believe this is happening to me." All those years working in a funeral home, and not once did I bring back a ghost. Move across the country and into a house like this, and *boom*. I have myself a Casper.

Naming him does nothing to calm the edge of my frayed nerves.

"Well, I mean..." She clears her throat. "At least he hasn't tried to hurt you. A ghost that plays the piano? That sounds like a friendly one."

"Or one that wants attention," I say as I drop my hand back to my side. My eyes zoom to the picture of Neil by the cheval mirror. I tilt my head. Stuck to it, partially tucked in the frame, is a rose petal. I frown as I stride to it.

Plucking it off, I bring it to my nose and take a whiff. I roll it in my fingers. It's still soft and smells fresh. *How the hell did this get here?* Finding them around the house is…well, it's not normal, but it's explainable. But stuck in a picture? I sure as hell didn't put this here.

Tori is saying something in my ear, but I don't listen. Instead, something shifts in the reflection of the mirror, and it gathers my attention.

From where I stand, in the reflection of the mirror, is the pasture. It's dark, and even though the moon isn't bright, I can still see him, the man standing by the patch of wild-growing roses. Arms loosely at his sides. His body turned in the house's direction. His eyes solely on me.

"Are you even listening to me?" she asks impatiently.

"Tori," I say on a breath as if it was knocked from my lungs. Fear so great spikes through me that it makes every hair on my body stand on end and every nerve ache. It may be a little bit of a distance, and it may be full of shadows from the maple trees, but I see him clear as day. The man in the picture. The man whose stepbrother thinks is missing. The man whose stained blood is all over my living room floor.

"What?" she asks after a moment.

A quick glance at the picture, and I know I'm looking at Neil Wordon. But when I look back, he's gone.

I scramble away from the window and scream.

A FIST BANGS on my front door, and I shoot off the old couch and dash to the door when Tori's voice directly follows.

"Tegan!" she yells as I fumble with the lock.

I swing the door open, and immediately, she shoves herself into the house and wraps her arms around me. "Are you okay?" she asks quickly. With her chin jiggling on my shoulder, I can tell she's wildly searching my living room. "Is he here? Have you seen him again?"

As I shake my head, we release each other. "No. He's been gone since we were on the phone."

Her little fingers turn into tiny fists at her side, and she gets a determined look in her sleepy eyes. She's still wearing her nightgown, and her short hair is in disarray, but she doesn't seem to care about her appearance as she demands, "Let me see the blood."

I swirl and take her to the edge of the rug, where I bend and lift it up. We look together, and eventually, she huffs a breath she must have been holding. "No one would survive that."

"You doubted me?" I drop the rug and stand back up with a scowl.

"Well!" She throws her arms up. "I had to see it for myself. I mean, no one could still be alive after losing all that blood."

"The FBI agrees with you," I say as I rake a hand through my hair.

"So," she begins, and I watch as she gulps a little, "you have a ghost then. Are you sure it's Neil Wordon?"

I head to the couch and pick up the picture I took

106

from the wall. Passing it to her, I explain, "It was him. I saw him. I know what I saw, and it was him."

She curses as she studies the picture. "Did you call the cops? You do have the sheriff's number."

"No!" I nearly shout.

She flicks her gaze back up to mine. "Why not?"

"What would I tell Sheriff Smith? That I saw his dead brother out in the pasture, hanging out with the roses? Oh, and he was in the house, watching me shower? And he's leaving rose petals for me to find?"

It can't be a coincidence that the rose petal was in his picture, and a few seconds later, I saw him standing by the roses. I know it was him that was bringing me the petals. It's a sick and twisted game, even for a dead guy.

"I don't understand the rose petals," she mumbles as she studies the pictures again.

"Ghosts like attention? Right?"

She shrugs and sets the picture back on the couch. "Yeah, I mean, why else would they make themselves known in weird ways?"

"Right." I nod fiercely. "I just won't give him the attention he wants."

She twists her lips a little, considering her next words. "You should try to find out what he wants."

"No!"

Gently, she takes my hand. "Tegan…"

I shake my head. "I left Chicago to get away from death, Tori. I left to change my life, so I will not be asking the ghost what he wants from me."

She scowls and drops my hand. "So you're just going to ignore him?"

"Yes." I nod. "With any luck, he'll get bored with me."

She giggles, but there's zero humor in it. "Right."

"I mean it, Tori," I add with determination. "I'm sorry he died, but I won't be engaging with him."

"You should really tell the cops," she whispers.

"Not going to happen." I remember how the sheriff treated me when I suggested the place was haunted. I won't be making that mistake again. "They'd think the new girl is crazy."

"Yeah, but maybe they could get some sort of priest or something to bless the house. And who knows, maybe somehow it'll help their investigation."

I point a finger at her. "That's if they believe me and don't lock me up instead. Somehow, I don't think the sheriff will be happy when I tell him I saw his brother's ghost."

She wrinkles her nose. "No, probably not." With a sigh, her shoulders deflate. "I'm sure I have something to ward off spirits at the shop. Somewhere in one of the boxes. If I can find it, you can have it."

"Really?" I ask hopefully.

She nods. "We can look for it in the morning when you come in."

I close my eyes and breathe a sigh of relief. When I open them, she has a little smile on her face. "Thank you, Tori. I mean it." I don't believe much in the Wiccan nature of things, nor do I believe much in an almighty God, but who am I to knock something that could possibly help me?

Her smile turns sympathetic, and she reaches to squeeze my elbow. "Anything to help. I'm going to go home and try to get some sleep." She wraps her arms around her middle, a little unsure as she glances around the living room. "You should try to, too."

I shake my head. "There's no way I'm going back to sleep. Besides, it's nearly morning."

"What are you going to do instead?" she asks with a cock of her head.

Wincing because there isn't a lot to do in this house, I say, "I have no idea."

"Well, good luck with that." She turns to leave, but with a look over her shoulder, she asks, "Bring coffee in the morning?"

I nod. "And a donut?"

Her smile puts me at ease. "You sure do know the way to my heart."

And with that, she heads out the door. I lock it as soon as it shuts and turn back to my empty house with a huff. I may be refusing to go back to bed, but I won't let death rule my life anymore.

"You can go to hell," I whisper to Neil Wordon, wherever his ghost is now.

CHAPTER 12
COLE GARNER

When I see her car parked outside the donut shop, my heart skips a beat. It's a strange feeling, this new sensation brought on by just the thought of seeing another person. A person I happen to surprisingly like.

I spent the night doing push-ups until I couldn't lift myself anymore just to clear my head. But, no matter how many I did, she occupied my thoughts. Her wit. Her smile. Her body.

Shutting the truck off, I chew on the inside of my lip for a second. I have no idea what *this* means, but my sister would have wanted me to explore it, to roll with it. I know she would have, and I can almost hear her little voice telling me to do it. So, when I finally went to bed last night, I decided to heed my dead sister's wishes and give in a little…to whatever this is.

Hopping out of my truck, I head inside the shop. I still haven't bought a coffee machine, but after the coffee yesterday morning, I craved it today.

My heart leaps again because I see Tegan right away. She's standing at the register, laughing with the owner of the shop as she gathers Tegan's order. Her laughter is like music, just like the sound of her moans.

This donut shop has been here since I was a child, but my foster parents never treated us to it. Thankfully, the owner took pity on us, and if we stopped by after school, she'd give us a day-old cookie to share. We'd eat it quickly, even before we left the shop, so that our fosters never found out that we were given handouts.

They were fond memories then, ones I held onto as I lived in prison, but now that I'm out, I realize how much bullshit they were. We deserved better. *She* deserved better.

Tegan is wearing another tank top today, but I can tell by the outline along her back that she's also wearing a bra this time. For a second, I let myself remember what she looked like without it. Standing before me, no shirt, no bra. Eyes hooded and full of lust.

My eyes lower to her jean-clad ass, remembering how her ass moved in my palms with each thrust.

She must feel eyes on her because she turns, and when she sees me, she smiles in greeting. I approach with a small smile of my own, but it fades when I take in her features. She has dark circles under her eyes, and as I get closer, her smile turns into a tired one, shaky around the corners.

"Here's your coffee, dear," the owner says. Tegan shifts her upper torso and thanks her, picking up both coffees and a white paper bag of donuts with the shop's logo stamped on the side.

The owner looks at me expectantly, so I raise a finger and say, "One coffee. Black."

As soon as she gets to work, I turn my attention to Tegan with a frown. "What's wrong?"

"What do you mean?" she asks with a lick of her lips. For a second, her eyes roam my chest apprecia- tively. I'm wearing another cutoff, and it shows some of my chest. I hadn't missed when she checked me out in the hardware store, and though I didn't wear this for her, I'm glad I did. I'd tease her for her visual explo- ration if she didn't look so damn exhausted.

"You look like you haven't slept."

She raises her gaze to mine and blinks tiredly before sighing. "I just need coffee."

Concerned, I reach and brush the back of my knuckles against her cheek. It was almost instinctual— to touch her. And I know I made the right move when she leans into it and exhales slowly. That one action, that little lean, makes my stomach do flip-flops. I have the urge to rub at the sensation, but instead, I ask, "Is this about yesterday?"

A scowl lowers her eyebrows into her blue eyes. "Like, *what* we did?"

I nod and glance at her neck. There are no bruises. It wasn't my intention to leave permanent marks, so I'm relieved when I find none. However, I do miss the red prints. Daydream about them, in fact.

She shakes her head. "No, no, not at all. That was…" She pauses to peek up with a grin. "More than I imagined."

I smile with her. "What were you expecting?"

"Well, for starters, I just wanted to go into the day trying to be your friend." She takes a sip of her coffee to hide the laugh bubbling up in her chest.

I laugh for her. "Sorry."

A blush colors her cheeks. "Don't be sorry. If we were alone, I'd ask for a repeat."

My cock stiffens in my jeans. There's no way in hell I'd deny her that.

"Is that so?" I rumble huskily. I have the urge to move in closer, but there are a lot of people here. I'm not sure if she'd appreciate a rumor spreading that she was getting cozy with me.

She lowers her coffee and bites her bottom lip, and it's then that I know she's thinking about it. About *what* we did. About us fucking and my hand around her neck and how most women would have run. Instead, I could tell that she liked it, got something out of it, just like I did.

I chuckle as her eyes flick to my cock. Whispering, I say, "You're wearing your thoughts out in the open, sweetheart."

She glances away, and her cheeks brighten even more. "Am not."

My humming in disagreement causes her to return her gaze to mine. "All you have to do is ask."

I watch as her eyes search mine, finding a deeper meaning, probably. Honestly, I don't know if there is one, but I do know that I want it as much as she does.

"I can't today," she eventually whispers. "At least, not until tonight. And…" She swallows nervously, and that causes the frown to return to my face. "I have something I want to talk to you about."

"What about?"

She clears her throat and glances around to make sure we aren't being overheard. "The house."

The owner of the shop hands me my coffee, and I dig out the amount from my pocket and hand it to her.

My frown only deepens when I turn my attention back to Tegan. I steer her away from the cash register a few feet. "And we can't talk about that here?"

She shakes her head.

"Okay," I say after a moment. "I'll stick around at the house and wait for you."

"Thanks. I—"

"Ms. Adams," a familiar voice says.

I close my eyes in blatant irritation. *Fucking great.* This is not what I wanted, and if I had seen his car outside, I wouldn't have come in.

Tegan turns to Smith as he waddles over to us. "Hi, Sheriff."

Smith completely ignores my presence as he smiles too wide with those crooked-ass teeth. He pats his belly, which I'm sure is brimming with donut holes. "I have a proposition for you."

"Oh?" Tegan says, checking the clock on the wall. She's probably late and doesn't have time for one of Smith's conversations.

"The wife and I own a cabin in the Ashley Forest."

"You don't say?" Tegan asks hurriedly.

"It's true," he says, nodding. "The misses and I were talking, and we thought it would be nice to invite you fishing up there sometime. You know, show you

114

what this area has to offer." He leans in a little, and I fight the urge to growl. I just know he's asking so that he can get her away from me and poison her mind. "She needs some friends, I think."

"Oh," Tegan says, drawing out the word. "Um. Maybe? I'm pretty busy right now."

Disappointment causes him to scowl a little, and I can't help but smirk. Did he really think that she'd just agree right away? Who the fuck would want to spend a few days fishing with the sheriff and his lonely wife?

Oddly, I feel possessive of Tegan. I could feel it in the tightness of my chest when he first uttered the invitation, but I could tell that Tegan was completely disinterested in it. Either she doesn't like to fish, or she doesn't want to spend time with them. Both could be true. Either way, it makes me feel fucking delighted.

"Sure, sure," he says. "Well, there's plenty of time for that."

Tegan nods and then looks at me from the corner of her eye. I decide to take pity on her. "Don't you have to get to work?" I ask.

She nods again, this time more vigorously. "I do. Um, it was nice talking to you, Cole. See you at the house?"

I wink at her, an indication of the promise of fucking her, and when she leaves, blushing, Smith turns a glare in my direction. "I don't want you anywhere near her."

My eyebrows raise. "That's not up to you."

"She's a good girl," he hisses, his cheeks reddening. "And if you weren't standing there, she would have agreed to some time away from you."

I stuff my free hand in my pocket. "If you weren't standing there," I throw back in his face, "she wouldn't have needed me to make an excuse for her to leave."

His eyes narrow even more. "You're sweet on her, aren't you?"

The way I roll my eyes is as dramatic as he's being. "Who I happen to like is none of your business."

"She doesn't need you tainting her. Does she know about your past?"

I shrug a little, refraining from saying that she only knows a small portion of it.

He pokes a finger in my direction, stopping inches from touching my chest. "She has a right to know, and if you don't tell her, I will. She should know who she's dealing with, of the prick who's trying to get in her pants."

"Are you saying that because of what I did to your cousin? Or because you think she needs to be tucked under your wing?"

His entire face reddens this time at the mention of his cousin. "Both," he says through clenched teeth.

"Right." I rock back on my heels and exhale with a smirk. "Do your worst, Smith, but I get the feeling she likes to make decisions for herself."

"We'll see, Garner. When she finds out what kind of man you are, she'll come running to me and mine, begging us to put you back where you belong. You're a murderer, and sooner or later, she's going to know all about your dark and twisted past."

And with that, he turns on the heel of his boot,

shoves the shop's door open, and strides out to his car. I stand there, watching him go, wondering if, by chance, he might be right.

Because I am a murderer. At the age of seventeen, I was arrested for manslaughter. And secrets like that don't stay secret for long in a place like this.

CHAPTER 13
COLE GARNER

S he had arrived looking even more exhausted than when I saw her that morning. I had barely stood up from fixing a cabinet door when she started in on what she wanted to tell me. Her words were slow and tired, and I listened intently as she explained how she thought the house was haunted and who it was haunted by.

I have to admit, I was a little shocked by everything that goes on here at night, but I also admit to finding a few rose petals here and there. I just thought she enjoyed picking them. Some women are weird like that.

Now, she rubs her face, giving me a moment to collect my thoughts. I have never put much weight into ghosts, but I also don't think Tegan is the crazy type. I believe she saw something, and I believe that she believes it was Neil Wordon from beyond his death.

She drops her hands down at her sides and blinks hard. "You believe me, don't you?"

I shift my weight from one foot to the other and then prop a hip against the counter to keep my fidgeting from being too obvious. "I believe you," is all I say.

Her shoulders sag in relief, and she looks down at my shoes. "Tori does too. I don't know if I can take much more death."

I scowl. "What do you mean?"

Her gaze flicks up to mine. "I worked at a funeral home before I up and left Chicago. I quit when the director made me work and attend my parents' funeral at the same time."

My expression widens before I blow out a breath. I can't imagine what that had to feel like. I found out my sister was dead through the grapevine. But to work her funeral and lay her to rest? I would have refused. It takes a certain kind of prick to force Tegan to do that.

She scrubs her face again. "Just a lot of death. It's no real surprise that I'm terrified of it."

"Everyone dies, Tegan," I say quietly. "It's only a matter of when and how."

She drops her hands back to her sides once more. "Yeah, well, I'd rather not die at all."

I smile a little. "Live immortally?"

"If I can help it, yes."

I cock my head to the side. "Why are you so terrified of death?"

The way she bites her lip, I can tell that she's thinking about how to word her answer. I wait patiently. "When you look into someone's eyes, you see life. A soul. Their thoughts in their expressions. There's someone *in* there, occupying the body. When they die, all that's left is the body. There's no soul. There's no someone *in* there."

"You're afraid of where they go? Where you'd go?"

She nods. "I love life too much to give it up to an unknown. For all I know, we just…disappear. Gone. Cease to exist. Float away and never live again. Never taste again. Never feel or love or hate again. We're just…gone forever. Like we were never there to begin with."

I nod as her words sink into me. I never thought of it that way, to be honest. Death has always been death. I can see why it terrifies her.

Seeing how much this subject upsets her, I go to her and pull her against my chest. I hadn't planned on it, on comforting her, but it just happened.

With my chin on top of her head, I murmur, "Well, you're still young. You have a long time before you can really start worrying about dying."

"Except for the fact that I'm being haunted by it." She chuckles even though we both know it's not funny. "Why me? Why can't I escape all aspects of death?"

"I don't know," I answer honestly.

"Tori wants me to go to the police, but I can't."

I grin a little, thinking of her calling the sheriff and trying to explain all this. "I don't think they'd believe you. Especially Smith."

She grips my cutoff like a lifeline. "So, I have to live with it then?"

Pulling back a little, I hold her jaw and tip her face up to mine. I don't have an answer, let alone a solution for her, so I press my lips to hers. She groans her approval against my mouth and slides her hands up under my shirt, running her fingertips over my abs.

For a second, I'm reminded of what Smith warned me of. Of telling her. I could easily do so now, but I find that I can't. If I do, she'll see me a hell of a lot differently than she does now. She's the only one who looks at me like I'm not who I am and sees me as someone who isn't defined by his past. If I tell her, she won't kiss me. Confide in me. Show trust in me.

Instead of giving in to Smith, I sweep my tongue against the seam of her lips. She opens immediately for me, and our tongues explore each other's mouths. My cock stiffens when she moans again. That damn sound. It'll be the death of me. I'll never get enough of it.

I sweep a hand over her curves until they rest against her ass. She scoots a little closer to me, her stomach now firmly pressed against my erection. I squeeze her ass in approval.

Reaching between us, she dips her hands into my shorts and grabs hold of the base of me. I jerk once at the sudden pressure and then rumble a groan into her mouth.

This wasn't my intention, instigating sex, even though I had promised it at the donut shop. My intention was to distract her from me giving her an answer to a problem I didn't know how to fix. But I'll never say no to sex, not with her. She's addicting, and I want more than anything to bury myself in that sweet, tight pussy of hers.

Dying to do it all day, I lower my hand from her jaw and wrap my fingers around her throat. She melts against me, and my suspicions are confirmed that she likes it when I take control like this.

I back her against the counter and squeeze a little. "Do you want me to fuck you, sweetheart?" I ask as I pull back a fraction.

She bites her bottom lip and nods.

Growling in satisfaction, I let her go and yank off her tank top. She pulls down her pants and kicks them aside until she's standing before me in nothing but a matching blue lace bra and panties. I remove my shirt before my lips are back on hers, my hands expertly flicking the clasp of her bra. She pushes down her underwear without being asked and without breaking the kiss.

It feels like fucking fire and ice at the same time when she explores the dips and slopes of my back. And when her hands slide lower and hook into the waistband of my shorts, I grind against her. It's not enough though, that pressure against my cock. I need her coming around it, her walls pulsing and tugging on it.

Angling her head back to deepen the kiss, she pushes my shorts and briefs down, and they drop to my ankles. I kick them aside, grab her hips, and hoist her onto the wood counter. She squeals into my mouth, and when she's settled, I break the kiss and spread her legs wide to get a good look.

"So fucking gorgeous," I rumble before I crouch and settle my face between her thighs.

Her breathing goes ragged, and when I flick my tongue out and swipe it against her clit, she inhales sharply.

I look up at her as I lick again, watching as her eyes blaze and her fingers grip the edge of the wood tightly. I keep eye contact as I swirl my tongue around the tight little bud begging for affection. Her hips buck against my face, but I grab hold of her thighs to keep her ass on the counter.

And then I feast, flicking and swirling and sucking.

The sounds that she makes have precum gathering at the tip of my cock. She tips her head back as I suck her clit into my mouth again and flick my tongue. Her hands fly to the back of my head to keep me in place, to tell me that this is what she wants and to not stop. I have no fucking plans to. Not until I taste her cum against my tongue.

Fingers rake against my scalp, and I growl against her. The vibrations only serve to make her legs shake around my head.

"Please, Cole," she says, looking back at me again. Her eyes are wide, begging and pleading. "Please."

I let go of one of her thighs because I'll never deny a lady who begs to come. Certainly not this particular lady.

Slowly, I insert a finger and crook it to hit her G-spot. I apply pressure as I rub the bundle of nerves. At the same time, I pick up pace with my tongue against her clit.

Her moans build and build, and her legs shake against my cheeks. The walls of her pussy tighten around my finger, and then she shatters, crying out my name as she comes along my finger. I ride the waves until her shaking reduces to trembles, and then I rise, sliding my finger out and sticking it into my mouth.

She watches with hooded eyes as I clean her sweet cum off my finger. I close my eyes to it, committing the taste to memory, and when I'm done, when my finger is clean, I bring her hips to the edge and press against her entrance.

"Ready, sweetheart?" I ask because, even though we've fucked before, I know there will be pain again. Pain that I get off on. Pain that I know she gets off on too.

She bites her bottom lip and nods, and that's all the approval I need before I slam into her. Her scream erupts into the kitchen, and I groan as tears line her eyes. Sweet tears. Tears that I caused. It fucking thrills me.

My grip on her thighs is nothing short of desperate, and I pull out and push back in before I know she's ready.

A sob escapes her, but I wrap my hand around her neck just to let her know that I'm in control, that I can give her pain or pleasure. Tears spill down her cheeks and drop onto my wrist as I move quicker, but after almost a minute, her sobs turn into deep moans.

I squeeze my hand tighter around her neck, enjoying how her face reddens, how I control how much she breathes, how much pleasure she takes.

Her eyes meet mine, and the trust I see in them

makes me groan. I don't deserve that trust, but she's giving it to me anyway. Submitting to it. I capture her mouth as I truly start to fuck her. Her breathing is ragged, breath fanning my cheek in short gasps. It only serves to fuel me.

The sound of how slick she is, sliding along my cock, and her thighs slapping against my hips fills the room. Our moans are joined as they spill into our mouths as we kiss. "So fucking tight," I say against her lips.

I slam into her harder, the wood on the counter groaning from the abuse. Her fingers dig into my sides, a pleasurable bite of pain.

Soft mewls escape her, and she closes her eyes in pure fucking bliss. The sight of it alone nearly sends me over the edge.

She's gorgeous. In this vulnerable moment, she's a fucking wet dream. I want nothing more than to run my hands along every curve, to lick my way over every thick inch of her. I don't know if we'll ever have the time to do that, if our moments will ever be raw enough for that, but a guy can dream that he's earned such rewards.

Her pussy ripples around me, and a tingle begins at the base of my spine. I drive into her, chasing both her and my release. Body trembling, short gasping breaths spill out of her until she screams. Her fingernails cut into my skin as her walls ripple and tug at my cock. The warmth of her cum spreads all over me, and I release her neck, grab her other thigh, and slam into her three more times before I explode with a shout.

My breathing is ragged as I slow my pace,

pumping everything into that sweet little pussy. And when we both come down from our high, I tip her head back and press a few kisses to the red marks I left behind.

"Fuck," she sighs when I move my kiss to the edge of her lips.

I chuckle as I slide out, head to the paper towels sitting on the counter, and bring them back to her. Gently, I clean her up, throw away the soaked paper towels, and help her to her feet.

We both get dressed in silence as we work to bring our breathing back to normal. When we're finished, she goes to me and curls her body against my chest, a hand tucked under her chin and her cheek pressed against my heart.

I wrap my arms around her and give her what she needs, even though I don't fully know what I'm doing. Comforting her is foreign to me—comforting *anyone* is something I haven't done in a long time—but I'm riding on pure instinct at this point. I must be doing something right, though, because not once has she complained about the holding, kissing, and stolen touches.

"You have to leave, don't you?" she asks quietly.

I glance outside and see the stars floating beyond. "I should."

She looks up and rests her chin against my sternum. "Will you stay the night?"

My eyebrows raise. I have never stayed the night with a woman before. In my teens, there was a lot of sneaking around. A lot of fucking and leaving before we were caught.

"Please?" she begs when I say nothing. "I don't want to be alone tonight, and I'd feel a hell of a lot safer with you around."

I hide it well, but my jaw flexes. She may trust me to keep her safe, but if she knew what I had done when I was seventeen, I doubt she'd feel the same. The thought nearly guts me.

Instead of voicing any of that, I give one curt nod and watch as she relaxes her shoulders in relief. "Thank you," she sighs out.

I flex my jaw again, reality hitting me square in the chest as she curls against me once more. Even if I never tell her, even if she never finds out, which would be a goddamn miracle, I know I'm not good enough for her. I'm not what she deserves, even if she thinks so.

I rest my chin against the top of her head, though, because tonight I can pretend otherwise. Tonight, I can give her what she needs and make her feel safe. Even if she will be lying with someone who has ended a life, whose hands had been so slick with blood that they couldn't hold a knife.

When she grabs my hand, I follow her to her bedroom. "Shower?" she asks once we're inside and she shuts the door.

I nod as she heads to the bathroom, traveling over a floorboard that creaks. Frowning, I walk to that spot while she turns on the shower. If I had known the floor creaks in here, I would have done something about it.

Crouching, I press on the board that squeaks. It wiggles a little, and my frown deepens. There's enough of a gap that I can squeeze something in between the boards and pull it up.

Curious enough to find out, I glance around the room and find a comb on the dresser. I grab it and return to the floor, sliding it between the cracks and popping it up.

"The fuck?" I whisper as I set the board aside. Tucked into the floor is a binder. It's covered in a layer of dust, but that doesn't stop me from pulling it out.

"What'd you say?" Tegan asks, popping her head out of the bathroom. When she sees me holding the binder, she steps fully out and into the bedroom. "What is that?"

"I don't know," I say honestly. The binder is zipped shut, so I open it. The sound of the zipper slices through the room, and I lay it on the bed as I flip it open. Layers of legal agreements and contracts slide around, and I glance at Tegan as she looks with me.

"Are those Neil's?" she asks as she picks up what looks to be a contract.

His name is on it, and I recognize the name of the other person who signed it. "Looks like it. This is one of the rentals that he owned. Now it's Derek's, but this looks to be Neil's shit."

"Hmm," she hums with a frown pulling her eyebrows together.

I take the paper from her and put it back into the binder. "We shouldn't be looking at this."

"Probably not," she agrees distractedly.

I zip the binder back up. "You should turn this in to the cops."

"Why?" she asks.

I look at her expectantly. "Because there could be evidence in here that can put his case to rest."

"Right," she whispers. "Okay. I'll turn it in."

Nodding, I drop the binder on the dresser and shuck my shirt. Steam is billowing from the bathroom, inviting me in. As I head to it, I glance back at Tegan, who is still standing there, staring at her bed where the binder once was.

"Coming?" I ask, pausing in my step.

She blinks, shakes off whatever thoughts are flitting through her mind, and looks over at me with a smile. "Yeah."

CHAPTER 14
TEGAN ADAMS

I gently wake and, with my eyes still closed, I nestle into my pillow and smile a little to myself. I haven't slept this well since before my parents died. All night, I was inside a cocoon that was Cole. His arms were wrapped around me, keeping me warm and giving me a sense of safety. I didn't dream about death. I didn't wake to the sound of Neil's ghost. My sleep was peaceful and undisturbed.

My smile fades because, even though Cole spent the night last night, he probably won't tonight. This is temporary, I remind myself, because he and I are not a couple. He has no obligation toward me.

I had asked him to stay in a moment of weakness. I was exhausted and not thinking clearly, and by some miracle, he agreed to it. That doesn't mean it'll happen again. He took pity on me, knowing I was weary and running on little sleep.

"There's nothing more happening between us," I whisper to myself as I snuggle deeper into the pillow for comfort. Even though I know that, deep down, I want there to be something between us beyond some serious attraction, I can't let myself have hope. I like Cole. He's a good person underneath all that surliness and secrets that are probably so dark I can only guess at them. We may not have gotten along when we first met, but I quickly realized there was more to him than met the eye. Except, you know, the giant secret: his reason for going to prison.

That's it though, isn't it? Nothing can happen between two people where there's a secret between them. And the fact that he hasn't told me yet makes me believe that it's bad. That it's unthinkable. However, I do deserve to know who is fucking me on what seems to be a regular basis.

A little annoyed at my thoughts, I flop over and stare hard out the window. Fog has settled over the land, so much so that I can't even see the tilting barn. No birds chirp. No horses neigh.

And Cole? He isn't lying there, but somewhere in the house, I can hear him walking around. He's probably working, and I find that I'm a little disappointed that he didn't stick around in bed with me. But again, we aren't anything. Not a couple. Likely just friends.

I flip on my back and drape an arm over my eyes. I'm an idiot. An idiot because that thought alone gives me horrible bad butterflies. They pang against the inside of my stomach, creating havoc on my emotions.

I breathe deep and exhale slowly. And then do it again. When I feel like I have a grip on myself, I drop my arm back to my side and fixate on my dresser.

On top of my dresser is the binder Cole found last night. I may have said that I'd turn it in to the cops, and I will, but I want to look through it first. If Neil's going to haunt me, I want to know more about him, even if it's all just legal documents. However, it raises a lot of questions about why it was under the floor in the first place.

What could have possessed him to put it there? Why hide it so well? I'll probably never get that answer, but I'm curious enough about its contents to shove back the quilt and head to the dresser.

With the binder in hand, I sit on the edge of the bed and unzip it. Carefully, I flip it open. I move aside the contract I read last night. There are a few other contracts between Neil and people I don't know, rental agreements it would seem, so I move them aside as well.

My eyes widen with what I find next. "A restraining order?" I whisper as I gently pick it up. Curiosity fully piqued, I quickly read it.

The restraining order is for my landlord, Derek. Neil was going to put a restraining order on him due to some vandalization and threats. I drop the hand holding the paper and frown at the adjacent wall.

I knew they didn't get along, but things got so heated between them that Neil was going to put a restraining order against him? The document was never turned in. It's still in the packet you fill out to give to a judge.

The big question is: Why didn't he turn it in? Why didn't he go forward with it? And another big question is what the hell did Derek do or say that made Neil feel he needed protection?

A horrible feeling settles in the pit of my gut. Whatever it was, Neil felt threatened by his own brother.

A sound outside my bedroom quickly shoves my thoughts aside. In what can only be the kitchen, I hear Cole curse as a pan hits the ground. I nearly jump out of my skin, having been so lost in thought that, for a moment there, I forgot Cole was even in the house.

I quickly assemble the papers the way I found them and zip the binder back up. Then I get up and dig in my top dresser drawer. When I find the tote bag I'm looking for among the mismatched socks and cute underwear and granny panties, I snap it open and slide the binder inside. I won't be turning this in to the cops today. Instead, I'm working at Tori's shop, helping her put the final touches before opening next week. You bet your ass that, on our downtime, we're going to go through this binder more thoroughly. I know I won't even have to ask Tori to help. She'll want to see all the dirty details for herself.

The tote thumps on the edge of the bed as I flop it down. I quickly get dressed, sliding on jeans and a simple graphic T-shirt. Socks come next, and then shoes. I may have cleaned up the dust and cobwebs, but that doesn't mean there aren't construction materials all over the house. I have no desire to ruin good socks even if they are mismatched.

I grab the tote and head out of the bedroom in search of Cole. I need to leave soon, but first, I want to talk to him to thank him for staying the night. I don't want him to think I'm ungrateful in any way. And I don't want him to feel like I'm using him for sex and security.

Cole's back is toward me as I enter the kitchen. He's hovering over the stove, and the scents of coffee and cooking eggs reach my nose and make my stomach grumble. My heart warms a little because Cole definitely doesn't seem the type to cook.

"Morning," I say. I step farther into the room and set the tote on the wood counter.

He peers at me from over his shoulder. His eyes are tired-looking, as if he literally got up minutes before me, and I find that completely sweet. He hadn't left me to work on the house like I thought. Instead, he left to make us breakfast.

"Are you making breakfast?" I ask.

He grunts as he pulls the pan of eggs off the burner. He dishes some out onto plates, grabs two spoons from the drawer, and heads to me.

"Thanks," I say, my heart skipping a few beats. He cooked me breakfast! I don't know whether to be impressed or feel guilty.

"I can't cook, so eat at your own risk," he murmurs, crossing the kitchen to the coffee pot and pouring the brew into two mugs.

He returns to my side and passes me one. I set my plate down next to the tote and take it gratefully. Around a bite of egg, I say, "It tastes good to me."

From behind the mug brought to his lips, he smiles a little. We eat in silence, and I watch him take every bite. Every now and then, he glances at me with a raised eyebrow. Eventually, he grunts, "You're staring."

I set my spoon down, my plate empty, and take a sip of my coffee. "I want some answers."

"About?" he asks as he slides the last bite into his mouth.

I nibble my bottom lip as I consider how to ask this, and when I find no better way than being direct, I sigh. "Why did you go to jail, Cole?"

He stiffens but tries to hide his discomfort by blowing on the steam of his coffee. "Does it matter?"

I shrug a little. "We are sleeping together. And I'd like to…um…consider us *friends*." That was hard to spit out, for some odd reason.

His mug quietly clunks as he sets it on the wood. "We can still be what we are without knowing everything about each other."

"I deserve to know," I say softly, fiddling with the hem of my shirt with my hand not holding the mug. "And from your mouth and not from someone in town."

His jaw flexes as he goes silent. I can tell he's struggling with himself, so I give him some grace and remain quiet. Eventually, he turns to me and rumbles, "Murder."

Murder. That one word rolls around in my head until it settles like a rock.

My eyes go wide, my feet rooted to the spot. But I don't run. Maybe a few days ago, I would have, but I know this man. Sort of. I think. "Murder?" I whisper, a little devastated.

He curtly nods. "I was seventeen."

"Who did you, uh…" I try to remain calm as I brush the hair from my cheek. "Kill?"

"His name was Rick Smith," he answers, his voice still rumbly. "My foster father."

I nod as though this makes total sense even though it doesn't. I realize then and there that I know nothing about Cole. Not a damn thing, so my voice is a little hostile when I ask, "Why?"

He turns and leans his ass against the counter while crossing his arms over his chest. "I had a sister."

"Okay…" I say, drawing out the word. "Like a foster sister?"

He shakes his head. "Biological."

"What do you mean, had?" I ask with a frown.

His glance in my direction is one full of pain, and I have the urge to try to comfort him, but again, I'm rooted to the spot. If I move, I could scare him from talking to me. I need answers.

"She killed herself while I was in prison."

My lips part, and a small gasp escapes. "I'm so sorry, Cole. What happened? Why did she—"

"Kill herself?" he interrupts when the word is too hard for me to spit out. I nod, and he sighs, resigned to the fact that I'm not going anywhere until the truth is out. "It's a long story."

"I can make time," I murmur.

Breathing deep, he begins. "It felt like every night Rick would sneak into her room."

My skin crawls, and dread fills me as my imagination runs wild. "To do what?" I ask softly, even though I know the answer.

He clenches his jaw. "To rape her."

136

I cover my mouth with my hand. "Oh my god."

"His wife knew what was going on. There was no way she didn't. My sister's crying filtered into my bedroom. She had to have heard it too."

I swallow with difficulty. "So you killed him?"

He looks at me and nods. "It started when she was ten and always happened around two in the morning. One night, a few days after my seventeenth birthday, I grabbed a knife from the kitchen and waited. He slipped into her room at the usual time, and I followed him in. My sister watched as I drove the knife into his back, yanked it out, and slit his throat."

My hand trembles, but I drop it back to my side and gently set my mug on the counter next to his. I don't have any siblings, but I can only imagine. "Why didn't you go to the police?"

He chuffs and looks away. "Smith, remember? Same last name as George Smith?"

"Oh god, the sheriff and your foster father were related."

He tightens his arms around his chest. "Cousins. I reported Rick on several occasions, but they never did anything. Not once."

"So you took it into your own hands."

"I did," he admits. He looks at me and searches my expression, waiting to find something. And then it hits me what exactly he's looking for: justification.

"I don't have any siblings, but I would have done the same thing, Cole." I would have. There's no doubt in my mind that I'd do the exact same thing if horrors like that happened to someone I loved.

I watch as his throat constricts when he swallows. "If I could, I'd do it all over again."

My heart breaks, and suddenly, murder doesn't seem so bad. He deserved more than a quick death, but it literally explains everything about Cole. Why he's so secretive, why he barely talks, why he keeps to himself. No one helped him when he needed it most.

In a roundabout way, it also explains the choking, the need to control, even if it's the life of another.

I head to him, peel his hand out from where it's tucked under the other arm, and curl my fingers between his. "I'd help you."

He searches my expression again, looking for the lie, the doubt. "You really aren't afraid of me, are you?"

I shake my head. "No. You and your sister should have never been subjected to a life like that. There's not an ounce of me that blames you for what you did."

His shoulders relax a little. "If only the town thought the same."

I cock my head to the side. "Do they know what Rick did?"

He shakes his head. "They don't seem to. For all I know, and by knowing Smith, it got swept under the rug, and I was made to be the guy who was covered in Rick's blood."

"Jesus," I breathe. And then I give his hand another squeeze. He squeezes back. "I don't care what they think. You know that, right?"

He nods a little. "I appreciate that."

"Does Derek know?" I ask curiously.

Lifting his other hand, he scratches at the stubble on his jaw. "He knows."

"And he doesn't care?"

He shakes his head again. "He wanted to stick it to his stepbrother."

I raise my eyebrows. I knew they didn't get along, but to hire a guy who murdered his stepbrother's cousin because he doesn't like his stepbrother is a little cold. But I don't say anything on that because, if he hadn't, I'd have never met Cole. That thought makes me sad, the possibility of never knowing him.

Standing beside him, his hand in mine and the truth bared, I stare at his profile as I come to a single realization. One I've been avoiding. One I've tried denying.

I have feelings for this man. This murderer. This broken soul. This unseen soul.

And I don't know how he feels about me. I don't know if it's only one-sided. Sure, there are stolen, tender touches. Sure, there are longing looks. But so far, he's been a closed book. Maybe it was because of his secret. Maybe it's rooted in his childhood and his only family member committing suicide. Whatever the reason, I can't tell him how I feel. Not only is it not the right moment, but the last thing I want to do is pressure him, especially if I'm reading this entire situation wrong.

So, instead, I give his hand one last squeeze and remove my fingers from his. "Do you want me to hang out with you today? Help around the house?"

He gives me a look like I'm being ridiculous. "I don't need a babysitter or a caregiver."

"Right," I say quietly. He's been living with this on his own for his whole life. I can't expect him to lean on me. "Well, if you need me…" I hold out a hand expectantly.

"What are you doing?" he asks, frowning at my palm.

"Give me your cell."

His frown deepens, but he pulls it out of his shorts pocket, unlocks it, and passes it to me. It takes me seconds to save my number to his contacts. "There," I add, hopeful he'll actually use it. "Call me if you need anything."

I pass it back to him and lean to give him a kiss on the cheek. And then I grab my tote and reluctantly turn my back on the man who opened up his secret to me.

CHAPTER 15
COLE GARNER

I swing the door open to the hardware shop and breathe in the familiar scent of oil and rubber. A slight stinging aroma of paint tickles my senses, which is my destination today. I start to make my way toward the familiar aisle, but as soon as I step fully into the store, I stop in my tracks.

At the register is Tegan and the friend she was with the other day. I can only imagine that this other person is Tori, the woman she's always on the phone with. It's hard not to hear her conversations. Tegan is a bright person, and her voice can sometimes carry if she's excited or happy about something. It's not a bad trait. In fact, it's contagious.

I had almost forgotten that Tori's new shop is next door, so it's no surprise that they're here, but I just didn't expect to see Tegan so soon after this morning's confession. I thought I'd have more time to process.

Swiping a hand over my mouth, I debate whether I'm going to turn around and head out of the store or move forward and greet Tegan. There's no way walking past her won't draw attention. It's not that I want to avoid her completely. It's just that my past is my past, and telling someone like Tegan about it was hard for me. A little embarrassing, even. The entire town doesn't even know everything she now does. I've harbored it for so long that it'd become a scar, and I cut it open today and showed her the wound. I don't like to show weakness, and today I did just that.

I lower my hand, knowing that I can't avoid her for long anyway. I stride forward, and as soon as I do, Tegan looks over. A smile graces her full lips when she spots me, and I breathe a sigh of relief that she wasn't going to make this awkward after what I told her.

"Hey, you," she says. At the sound of her greeting, Tori looks up from sliding her card through the machine.

"Hey," I say, stopping just beside them. Tegan leans in and wraps one arm around my waist in a hug. I squeeze her for a second, and then we pull apart. It's hard not to miss how Tori studies it, the interaction. It makes me wonder what all she knows. How close are Tegan and Tori? Are they close enough to swap stories?

"What are you here for?" Tegan asks.

"Paint," I answer with a flick of my thumb north, the direction of Derek's rental.

"Oh," she says with a frown. "You could wait for me for that. Painting is actually the one thing I like to do."

I shrug. "Sure. I could work on landscaping today until you get home."

She smiles again and is about to say something else, but Tori clears her throat and gives us an expectant look. Tegan cringes through her smile. "Right. Tori, this is Cole. Cole, this is Tori, my best friend."

Tori holds out her hand, and I shake it, masking my surprise that it's a firm grip for such a dainty woman. I suppose it must come with the territory of a businesswoman.

If I had any illusions about what Tori knew about Tegan and me, they vanished as soon as Tori said, "You must be the boyfriend."

A shocked look wipes the smile right off Tegan's face. "He is *not* my boyfriend."

By this time, the cashier is glancing between us, clearly eavesdropping. I shift uncomfortably, both at the implication that Tegan is my girlfriend and the fact that we have a listener. I don't want anyone to think Tegan and I are together because the last thing she needs is for rumors to spread that she's saddled with a murderer. It's not that I don't want Tegan. In fact, the idea of it thrills me. But, surprisingly, I care too much about her to have her labeled.

"Could have fooled me," Tori says with a dramatic lift and fall of her shoulders. "You're making googly eyes at each other."

I scowl. Was I? I mean, I'm not oblivious to Tegan. I've seen her naked, and for a brief second, my eyes undressed her. Was it obvious? I must be losing my touch at hiding my expressions, and that thought only makes my scowl deepen.

"Am not!" Tegan hisses.

Tori looks over her shoulder at the cashier. "Am I wrong?" she asks of her.

The cashier only smirks, picks up a thick book from the counter, and pretends to be really interested in it.

"Tegan doesn't want me," I grunt.

Tegan turns a frown in my direction. "I don't?"

I shift uncomfortably again. "I'm not boyfriend material."

For a second, I see a hurt expression on her face, but she covers it quickly and nudges Tori's shoulder. "See? Not dating."

"Right. Only fucking," Tori mentions with a roll of her eyes.

Color splashes across Tegan's cheeks. "You're going to be the death of me."

"Right," I murmur, ready to bolt away from this conversation and the best friend that reads too much into things. "Well, I'll see you when you get off, Tegan."

And with that, I leave the girls. As I walk away, I can hear them bickering until their hushed voices cut off as they leave the store.

After I grab the paint and an employee to mix the color, I stretch out my tight shoulders. *Boyfriend.* Am I giving Tegan the wrong impression? How much is she telling Tori? How much does the town know? What do they think is going on?

The cashier heard everything. Although this is Mount Pleasant, it's only a matter of time before it spreads like wildfire into Fairview. What will they call Tegan? How will she fare with the rumors? Will she care? Will she be pissed? Will she demand that I stay away from her?

I grunt my thanks to the cashier as soon as I'm done charging the paint to Derek's account. The entire time, she gives me a knowing look, and it's then I know that the rumor has already begun. Everyone in this store knows me, and now they know Tegan. And thanks to Tori, they know Tegan and my business.

This entire thing is fucked.

My shove of the store's door is a little rough, but at this point, I'm a little pissed. Tegan doesn't deserve the shitstorm coming her way.

Distracted by my thoughts, I don't see Derek until he calls my name. I turn as I set the paint in the bed of my truck and watch as he lazily approaches. Today seems to be the day when I can't have a moment of peace, but I hide my curses under my breath well.

As he strides in my direction, he goes into a fit of coughs.

"How's the house coming?" Derek asks when he's right in front of me, his voice hoarse from coughing. He seems to be in a chipper mood for someone who looks like complete shit. He's even skinnier than when I saw him last, so much so that his clothes practically hang off of him.

"Good," I say. "Wallpaper is off, and I came for paint."

"Good, good." He crosses his arms loosely over his chest. "Is Tegan a big help?"

I narrow my eyes at him. "You could have told me she was a chick. You didn't have to hide that bullshit."

He grins. "Now where's the fun in that?"

145

I stuff my hands into my pockets. Honestly, I'm not mad about it, just annoyed that he thought he could play games with me for his own entertainment. "Tegan is useful, yes." More than useful. Hot, sexy, and willing, but there's no way in hell that I'm going to give him that information. He probably wouldn't like it very much.

"Wonderful," he says. Then he goes into another fit of coughs.

I wait until he's done before I side-eye him and ask, "Still no answers?"

He shakes his head. "Just came from the doctor when I saw you." He points to a few stores down. When I was younger, it used to be an office for the local pizza place. Since then, they built their own building on the other side of Mount Pleasant, and a doctor with a few nurses took over their old space.

"It doesn't help that they have to ship tests off to be analyzed, but he mentioned today that he's running out of tests to take."

"Did you try a bigger town?" The doctors should be better at a hospital.

"He said that, if he couldn't find answers with this last round of tests, he was going to refer me. I'm not looking forward to the drive."

I grunt in agreement, and he waves a hand in my direction before we switch topics.

"Did you find anything worthy of keeping in the house?" he asks.

I shake my head. "A lot of old shit, but nothing worth anything. Tegan found something, though." I don't mention it was me because he doesn't need to

146

know that I was in Tegan's bedroom. That would just lead to more questions because we both know the only reason I'd go in there was to remodel the bathroom, and that project hasn't started yet.

"Oh?" he inquires, lifting a bushy eyebrow above the wide rim of his glasses.

I curtly nod. "A binder that was your brother's."

Both of his eyebrows pinch together, and his arms tighten across his chest. "A binder of what?"

I shrug a little. "Looked like legal documents."

He's quiet for a moment, and I can see his mind racing. Eventually, he speaks, and it has so much conviction to it that my eyes widen a fraction in surprise. "You need to hand it over to me."

"Why?"

"Because I need to go through it," he says quickly. "My lawyer needs to see it."

"Tegan was going to turn it in to the police."

He shakes his head. "I'll do that after my lawyer looks it over."

My eyes narrow. "It's evidence, Derek."

His expression matches mine. "And the authorities will get it. After I've looked it over."

We stand there for a moment, in a battle of wills, but eventually, I roll my eyes because I know he won't give up on this. When Derek Wordon wants something, he always gets it. Who am I to care who falls into possession of legal shit? "You'll have to ask Tegan for it if she hasn't turned it in already."

"I guess I'll have to do that," he says defensively. I have the urge to protect Tegan because I don't like that look on his face. It's the look that he plans to bully to get what he wants. He's tried that a few times on me but has since learned that I don't respond the way he wants when he tries. I'll have to see to it that he doesn't bully Tegan, if anything, to make sure she's warned that he wants it.

And who knows, Tegan will probably hand it over without a problem.

"How about I get it from Tegan and give it to you?"

His jaw flexes as he thinks it over, and then he pushes up his glasses. "Sure. It'll save me a trip."

He lingers for a moment, his gaze searching the space behind me without really seeing. I clear my throat to draw back his attention. "Anything else you need?"

Snapping his eyes back to mine, he gives a quick shake of his head and begins to back away. "I should get going anyway. Tea with my stepbrother is boring as hell, but it does soothe the throat."

And it's free, I don't mention. Instead, I nod to him, grab the door handle of my truck, and pop it open. He waves me off as I hop, shaking my head as I do. For a man with a lot of money, he sure does have a lot of issues.

CHAPTER 16
TEGAN ADAMS

Tori's office isn't as small as I thought it'd be. For the most part, she's unpacked her office supplies and stuffed them away on proper shelves and in desk drawers. A few small boxes that were delivered yesterday are left, but they sit off in the corner, waiting to be put away.

Aside from the desk and shelves, she has a fluffy sitting chair that sits before a small round coffee table. Both look like they were found at a garage sale, but I couldn't care less. They're cute, and I would have picked them up myself. But that's where I sit, my sandwich on the table and Neil's binder next to it. Tori is behind her desk, munching away on a carrot while she fires up her laptop to do a little work during lunch.

Thankfully, since we arrived back at the shop from the hardware store, she let the topic of me and Cole's status lie to rest. At least, for now. I can tell she has a lot of opinions on the matter, but so far, she's refrained from voicing them. Until this moment, I didn't know she was capable of such restraint.

I still can't believe she called him my boyfriend. The shock has yet to wear off on the blurted accusation. At no time have I told her about my feelings for Cole, or what we share, or lack thereof. All she knows is that we've had sex a few times. Maybe she read between the lines. Maybe I implied that there was more. Either way, if she brings it up again, I'll have to set her straight.

"Did you see that new house for sale?" Tori asks as she squints at the screen of her laptop. "It's in Fairview. I just listed it yesterday."

Carefully, so that the loose lettuce doesn't spill out and onto the floor, I unwrap my sandwich. "No," I answer.

She swivels her laptop around, and I watch as the pictures flip by across the screen. It's a cute, one-story, white house with a couple of bedrooms, a master with a small but luxurious bathroom, an extra bathroom, and a nice kitchen complete with brand-new stainless appliances. Everything has been updated to perfection and is exactly the kind of house I've always wanted. "It's beautiful," I breathe as my heart sinks, knowing that this house will never be in the cards for me.

"It could be yours," she singsongs.

I roll my eyes even though I feel a little defeated on the subject. "There's no way I could afford it."

Her lips form a thin line, and she turns the laptop back to herself. "Right. It'll probably be on the market for a little while anyway. It's too fancy for a town like this, and therefore, too costly. But there's another house next to it. A little smaller, not as nice."

"And?"

She shrugs a little. "I could buy it and start my own rental business. Derek Wordon might be on to something there."

"Mm-hmm," I hum, turning back to my sandwich and lifting it to my lips.

Chewing on a bite, I unzip the binder and flip it open. I leaf through the contracts and read the restraining order one more time. I don't glean any more information than what I read before, but I just wanted to make sure that I saw what I saw.

The paper after that is the property's size, which happens to be ten acres, and after that, the vet records of what I can only assume is for the horses in the pasture. I have yet to go out and pet them. They never come to the fence anyway unless their owner shows up with carrots and apples. They're pretty, though, watching them roam the property at complete ease, unaware that their space is haunted. Or maybe they are aware and just don't care. Maybe it's the norm for them.

"What are you looking at?" Tori asks.

I glance up and watch her pop a slice of green pepper into her mouth while she looks at me expectantly. "A binder of Neil's."

Her eyebrows raise as she chews thoughtfully. "Any good gossip?"

I grin a little at her. "Depends on what you think is gossip."

She touches the tip of a celery chunk to her chin. "All right, spill the beans. What's in the binder?"

Grabbing the vet records, I hold them up and wave them around a bit. "Just legal stuff."

"And why do you have Neil's legal stuff?"

I scowl. "Finders keepers."

She blinks at me. "You're telling me you found something that the cops didn't?"

I nod. "In the floorboard."

Leaning forward, she rubs an eyebrow and sets her celery stick back into the container of mixed vegetables. "You should have turned that in by now."

I cringe a little and set the paper neatly back in the binder. "I plan to. Calm down."

She looks at me for a long moment before sighing. "I know you. You've pored over what you've found so far, and you have no intention of turning it over until you've seen it all."

"And your point?"

She circles a hand in the air. "Tell me what you've found."

I shrug a little. "An unfiled restraining order against Derek Wordon."

Her hand flops down to the desk. "Wait, seriously?"

I nod again. "I guess Derek was threatening him, although it doesn't say why. But according to everyone, they hated each other, so maybe that hate just grew."

"Normally," she begins, drawing out the word, "when siblings hate each other growing up, they either move far away from each other, or they learn to find common ground. Things don't escalate unless there's a reason."

"What do you think the reason was?" I ask as I turn over the vet bill to look at the next document. When I do, I suck in a breath.

"What?" she asks as I read the first paragraph.

I hold up a finger, and when I'm satisfied that I've read enough to know exactly what this is, I look up at her with wide eyes. "It's a living will."

Surprised, she juts her chin and then swiftly stands from her office chair and makes her way around the desk. When she's beside the coffee table, she squats to look at the paper with me. She quickly reads through, and after she's done, she turns a frown at me. "Neil left everything to his stepbrother?"

"It's crazy, isn't it?" I whisper, as though the walls have ears.

"Oh god," she whispers back. "This is bad, Tegan."

"Why?"

"Because," she says, setting the paper neatly back in the binder on top of the papers I haven't read yet. The way she handled it was as though it could combust at any given moment. "If the sheriff learns that everything Derek has is actually his, you could be out of a place to live. Hell, Cole will be out of a job *and* a place to live, because according to you, they hate each other."

"Shit," I murmur, looking at the binder as if it might bite me. "What do I do?"

"Well." She blows out a breath and stands fully

upright. "You can't turn that in. Not if you care about Cole."

I scowl. I shouldn't be surprised that she said that, but I am. "You want me to hide possible evidence from the authorities?"

"Yes," she says, bobbing her head. "At least for now."

"And if I get caught with the evidence?" I do see her point because, selfishly, I want to know everything about the man who died in that house and is now haunting me, but I also know, on some level, it's wrong.

"Look," she says, heading back behind her desk and taking a seat. "You have a choice to make. Either you pretend it doesn't exist to keep your place and Cole keeps his job, or you turn it over and have both of you lose everything."

The thought of Cole being homeless and jobless twists my insides. And I would be the one who would cause it. I'm not worried about myself. I'd find a way to survive, maybe even move in with Tori, but he would have nothing and nowhere to go. I couldn't do that to him. I couldn't be the reason he loses everything he's worked so hard for.

"Fuck," I grumble.

A sly smile is turned my way. "Exactly. Because you have feelings for him, you have to do what's right by him."

I snap my gaze at her. "I do not have feelings for Cole Garner."

She scoffs, and the chair squeaks as she leans back. "Oh, don't give me that shit. I know what you look like when you're smitten. You like Cole. Don't pretend otherwise. It's a little insulting."

Blushing, I glance away. "There's just a lot more to him than everyone thinks."

Out of the corner of my eye, I see her shrug a little. "I honestly don't know what other people think. I haven't asked around about him. All I know is that he went to prison, and he's gruffy."

I slide my gaze back to hers, squinting one eye. "Gruffy?"

She nods. "And grumbly."

I chuckle a little and flip the binder shut. "Yeah, he is, but he has his reasons."

"And those are…?"

My lips pucker. I lean forward, grab my sandwich, and take a bite so I don't have to answer. Can I lie to Tori? I never have before about big stuff like this. Would she know if I lied? I mean, I understand Cole's reason for what he did, but would Tori? We may be best friends, but we don't always agree on everything.

"Oh, come on, Tegan."

I chew and swallow, biding my time. When I see that she's not going to leave this alone, I sigh. "What he did to go to prison for was justified."

She raises an eyebrow, waiting for me to clarify. I don't, so she presses. "Is that all you're going to tell me?"

I shrug, and my tone is pitched higher when I explain. "It's not my story to tell, honestly. But all you have to know is that it's justified, and I would have done the exact same thing."

"I see," she says thoughtfully and, honestly, a little

doubtfully. Almost like she doesn't trust my judgment. Maybe she's right not to.

"He's a good guy, Tori." I feel compelled to defend him, to have someone see him for something other than what he shows on the outside. "You're going to have to trust me on that."

Elbows on the desk, she touches her hands together in a prayer position and taps the tips of her fingers to her mouth. "Just promise me something?"

I narrow my eyes. "I make no promises until I know what it is."

"Just don't get hung up on a guy who may be incapable of getting hung up on you."

My throat bobs as I swallow with difficulty. "How do I know, exactly, if he's incapable?"

Her shrug is small. "The only way to know is if you talk to him."

"And say what?"

She drops her hands back to the desk. "Just ask him where you two stand. If it's just sex and friendship or if he feels something more."

My shoulder suddenly feels tense, so I rub at it as I consider what she said. The more that I think about it, the more I know she's right. I have feelings for Cole, and I can either let them grow into something I can no longer control or learn where I stand when it comes to him. I deserve to know before I get so wrapped up in a guy that I'd get hurt if he walked away because I was nothing more to him than sex and friends.

"Okay," I nod. "I promise that I won't let my pussy lead me down the road of no return before talking to him about his feelings." Even as I say the words, I know it's not going to be an easy conversation to have.

She curtly nods and turns back to her laptop. "That's all I wanted to hear."

CHAPTER 17
COLE GARNER

Brows pinched in concentration, I swipe the wet paintbrush against the cabinet door when I hear a car door shut outside. As promised, I left the walls alone, but Tegan and I didn't discuss the cabinets. And since Derek is too cheap to buy new cabinets, I have to update the old ones.

A little paint goes a long way. They may not look new, but they look far better than what they did.

Leaning back on my heels, I survey my work. With updated hardware and new counters, whenever those come in, it'll look like a new kitchen. Sort of.

I've only tackled the base cabinets, however, but for an afternoon's work and several coats of paint, I'd pat myself on the back if I did that kind of thing.

This morning, I pulled the overgrowth in the front of the house. The mower I usually borrow wasn't available today to cut the grass in the back, so I was stuck doing the one job I hadn't been looking forward to since seeing the house. The front looks good, though. Under the baking sun, I pulled up every plant, but now it's up to Tegan to either leave it bare or pick out new plants.

The front door swings open, but oddly, it's tentatively closed. Quietly. Suspiciously, even. I know it's Tegan, though, because I hear her footfalls as they head toward the smell of fresh paint. By now, I know her gait.

The lid pops as I put it back on the can of paint. I set it aside, out of the way, before I move to wash my hands in the sink. It's almost dark; I've worked long enough.

I hear her enter the kitchen as the water is running over my hands. She doesn't say anything as I grab the soap bottle, squeeze some into my palm, and lather my fingers. In silence, I scrub at the mix of dry and wet paint along my skin.

The weight of her gaze on my back makes me frown. She has yet to say anything, so, curiously, I look over my shoulder as I rinse the suds off. She lifts her gaze to mine with a pinched expression.

"Hey," I murmur as I shut off the water.

"Hi." She loosely crosses her arms over her chest. Her tone was unsure.

Suspicious, I flick the water off my hands, and I turn to face her. I don't like how uncomfortable she looks. Is it because of what I confessed this morning in this very spot? Or did something happen at Tori's shop? "How was work?"

Her shoulders rise and fall as she takes a deep breath. "What are we, Cole?" she blurts.

My frown deepens. "What do you mean?"

159

Her arms tighten around her chest as she grows more and more uncomfortable. "I mean, you and me. Friends? Lovers? More?"

I prop my damp hands on my hips and glance down at my shoes. This isn't a conversation I thought we'd have, at least not so soon. "Is this because of what Tori said at the hardware store?"

I see her shrug from under my lashes. "Maybe. I —" She rakes her hands through her hair. "I don't know. I don't know anything, to be honest." She drops her hands back to her sides. "I just need to know what to expect here."

Leaning my backside against the sink, I say carefully, "I meant what I said. I'm not boyfriend material."

The space between her brows pinches together. "Why?"

I chew on the inside of my lip for a second as I think of how to tell her how I feel. Feelings have never been my strong suit, no matter how often my sister tried to get me to express them. It's hard to do that when you're protecting someone, once my sister, and now…"You deserve more than what I can offer."

She wraps her fingers around her other arm's bicep and thins out her lips. "I get to decide what I deserve."

I shake my head a little. "You just don't get it, do you?"

"Get what, Cole?" she asks on an exhausted exhale.

"You have no idea what it'll be like, saddled with me. I'm nothing more than a murderer to these people. Nothing more than an ex-con who went away before he could even legally buy a pack of cigarettes. Never mind my reasons for doing what I did because they have no idea. You know what they'll see you as?" I open my arms, embracing the town. "Do you have any idea what they'll say about you? How they'll look at you? What they'll label you?"

Her frown deepens, and she searches the space across my chest. As she comes to some sort of conclusion, she whispers, "I've never lived in a small town before."

I cross my arms. "That's my point. You have no idea what this will be like for you."

Her eyes narrow. "I get that you're trying to protect me, but I don't need protecting from people I don't know. Whispers are whispers. Rumors are rumors. As long as I know the truth, they can't touch me. I am not made of glass. I couldn't care less what they think or say about who I choose to spend my time with."

My lips purse. She's saying all the right things to make me give in, but she still doesn't get it. "I'm no good for you, sweetheart."

She takes a step in my direction. "Says who? Them?"

I have no real answer for that, so I just stare her down.

Another step in my direction. "Says you?"

I look away.

She had taken another step, and now she stands before me. I can feel the heat coming from her body, but I keep my arms crossed instead of reaching out and putting my hands on her like I want to. "They may have labeled you for what they believe you are, but they're not the only ones." I look back at her as she gently pokes my chest. "You've labeled yourself. Deemed yourself unworthy of living a normal life because of the shitty past life you had."

"And how would you know?"

"Because I know you. And because I came here thinking the exact same thing. I have a past too, Cole, and it isn't all blooming roses. It's weeds and thorns. Maybe not as horrendous as yours, in fact, nowhere near it, but it wasn't an easy life, especially when I ran away from it to start over."

I search her face, looking for a fib, a lie, a tall tale. I find nothing but sincerity. "What are you saying?"

"That you need to start over."

"And how do I do that?"

"Well," she begins, blowing out a breath. "Start by labeling what the hell this is between us."

I swallow with difficulty. "What do you want this to be?"

She bites her bottom lip but raises her chin with a certain sort of confidence that doesn't match her expression. "How do you feel about me? Don't think about it. Just say it."

"You're beautiful," I say automatically. It's the very first thing that popped into my head, and it felt right as soon as it left my mouth.

The blush along her cheeks is endearing, boosting my confidence, but she doesn't break our gaze. "And?"

I shrug a little, butterflies fluttering in my stomach. "You're cool. I like you."

"Well, that's good, since you don't seem to like anyone." She smiles shyly. "But in what way do you like me?"

Finally giving in to the urge, I reach forward and tuck a stray hair behind her ear. "In ways that I didn't think I was capable of."

Her red cheeks turn even brighter, and I find that I like that shade. I smirk as she whispers, "I like you too. A lot. And as more than just friends." She glances at our feet. "Way more than friends."

I tuck a finger under her chin and raise her gaze back to mine. The butterflies explode in my stomach, and I lean forward and capture her mouth. The instinct to do so is surreal because, not once, except for my sister, have I had someone care about me. They saw me for what was on the outside. First, a child from a broken home. Second, a foster child. Third, a lying child. Fourth, a murderer. Fifth, an ex-con. She doesn't label me. She sees me for who I am.

There was a time when everything meant nothing to me. In fact, that time was before Tegan came into my life. But she had, and she is. And even though I don't believe it's possible to actually start over, I'm going to give it a shot.

Because I care about her more than I can admit at this moment. More than the words I'm capable of understanding.

She kisses me back as I back her toward the counter, my crooked finger under her chin lowering until my hand is wrapped around her neck. She groans into my mouth, and I smile a little against her lips as we bump into the counter. Not only was it instinct to kiss her after her confession, but I have this dying need to seal it with sex. With being buried inside her. With telling her how I feel when my words lack impact.

I flip her over and press my palm into the back of her neck until she's bending over the wood counter. I rain little nibbles across the width of her shoulders as I hook my fingers into the waistband of her shorts and shove them down. Her breathing becomes more and more ragged with every single bite.

"Tell me what we are, Cole," she says between breaths.

I pause for a second. Then, in between bites, I say, "You're the only one I want to fuck. You're the smile I want to see every damn day. If you need to label it, then call yourself mine, sweetheart."

A shiver racks her body, and I shove down my paint-splattered shorts until my cock springs free. The cooler air of the house wraps around my shaft, but I grip it and press the tip against her entrance.

This will not be gentle. This will not be kind. This is a fucking need, a desire so damn deep that I'm convinced if I don't bury myself inside her, my world will literally fall apart.

I groan as I shove inside. While she screams at the sudden intrusion and bite of pain, her pussy ripples around my cock, and *fuck* does it feel so damn good.

Grabbing hold of her hips, I pull her ass back against me, pushing deeper inside. I watch as her fingernails scrape against the counter, and if it weren't for her moans punctuated by little sobbing hiccups, I'd take it easier on her. But my girl likes the pain, I know she does. She doesn't have to voice it for me to know.

It's in the slight arch of her back. It's in the way her pussy soaks me. It's in the tone of her sounds of pleasure.

"You look so pretty for me, sweetheart," I grit out as I begin moving inside her. Her cheek is pressed against the wood, but her tears glisten against her other cheek under the kitchen lights.

Her buckled knees begin to relax while I pump inside her, and I pick up my pace, fucking her the way I want to. I meant what I said, I realized with each thrust. She's mine. Just the thought of her doing this with another guy has me near rage. I don't want her with anyone else. I want her with *me*. Fuck the consequences. Screw the rumors. If she can handle them, then so can I.

Her moans deepen into the sound that drives me crazy, and her thighs begin to shake. I know she's close to coming, right on the edge, so I reach forward, wrap my hand around her neck, and choke her as I pound into her.

The deep moans are strangled, and her face turns a pretty shade of red, but with a few more pumps, her throat vibrates against my fingers as she attempts to scream. Her orgasm squeezes my cock so damn tight that the tingle slams into the base of my spine.

"Fuck," I moan. "That's it, sweetheart. *Fuck.*"

I let go of her neck, grab her hip, and slam so deep into her that I see fucking stars when I come. My head tips back as I pump everything I have into that sweet pussy of hers. When I finally spill the last drop, I gently ease out of her. Cum immediately drips down her thigh, but I pull up my shorts quickly and grab

165

some paper towels. Gently, I clean her up, throw away the paper towels, and carefully pull up her shorts. She lies there against the counter as I take care of her, trying to get her breathing under control.

Grabbing her hips, I gently turn her to face me. Her cheeks are wet from tears, so I wipe them away with my palms and then press a kiss to her mouth. Against my lips, she murmurs, "So we're a thing?"

I smirk and pull back. She just has to have the words come straight from my mouth, doesn't she? "If you feel the need to label it, yes, we're a thing." *Why do I like the sound of that?*

That's something I'll have to get used to, voicing my thoughts, because Tegan seems to need the verbal proof that goes along with the physical proof.

She smiles at me and adjusts her hair, untangling the knots that were brought on by leaning against the wood. As she does, her head turns to the right, and I watch as she frowns.

I look with her, and there, resting against the floor, is a rose petal. My frown matches her own as she asks, "I saw that you did the front, but did you mess with the rose garden too?"

"No," I grunt as I look back at her, remembering her ghost story. "But I keep finding those damn things everywhere, and I'm about to take a mower to them."

Her gaze is solely fixed on the petal, and the color that I had brought to her cheeks drains a little. I don't like the worry on her face, so I tip her face back to mine and press a small kiss to the corner of her mouth. "How about I take you up on your offer?"

"What offer?" Her scowl is adorable, but my words distracted her.

"Bowling." *Because I'm just not done with you yet.*

She laughs a little, but it doesn't reach her eyes. Glancing once more at the petal, she turns back to me and nods. "I'd like that."

Relieved, I let her go and crossed to the paint supplies to clean the brushes up before we head out for the night. As I do, out of the corner of my eye, I watch as she picks up the petal and quickly throws it away in the trash.

CHAPTER 18
TEGAN ADAMS

"*H*appiness is what you make of it, Tegan," Dr. Lynn said over the rim of his tea. "You decide what makes you happy, what makes you sad, what makes you angry. You decide how it affects you and the actions you take with it."

"Another strike!" I say, completely astounded. I don't know how Cole keeps getting strikes, but it's blowing my mind. How did he get so good?

At first, he kept getting gutters. The frustration on his face was evident. It was as if he'd never been bowling, and with his upbringing, I doubt he had even felt the weight of a bowling ball in his palm. But after a few turns, he seemed to have it down, knocking down pins in one go at it. He's a quick learner, and I shouldn't be surprised. I've learned not to underestimate Cole and not to think anything is impossible for him.

A wide grin spreads across his face as he spins and strides back to our booth in front of our alley. I can't help but grin back even though he's completely kicking my ass. I've never seen him smile. Smirk, yes, but this kind of smile? And have it directed at me? It has my stomach in happy little knots and my heart beating just a tiny bit faster.

He reaches me, places both hands on either side of my shoulders to grip the back of the booth, and bends to kiss me. I kiss him right back, not giving one shit who sees.

People are watching. They've been subtle or openly staring at us since the moment we walked in. I ignored them just like Cole did, and we grabbed an lane, kissed, and shared food like they didn't exist at all. I wasn't going to give him any reason to doubt what I had said at the house because I meant every damn word. I don't give a crap what they think about us. About me. About him. I didn't come here to be popular among the small population. I came here to escape a life of death, to escape who I was, to leave my fears behind, and I found all those in the man whose tongue is licking the seam of my lips.

"Last turn," he whispers against my mouth.

"I'm going to kick your ass," I lie.

He laughs, leans away, and sits down in the seat next to mine. He knows it's literally impossible for me to beat him, but I get up anyway, grab my borrowed bowling ball, and head to our alley with a certain cocky sway of my hips. I can hear his chuckle as I take careful aim, blow out a breath, and send it down the alley.

I cringe when every pin is knocked down but one

to the far left and one to the far right. *An impossible shot*.

Whipping back around in mock fury, I glare at my man. His lips are tucked between his teeth to hide the laughter that's making his shoulders shake. I force the amusement from my face, grab my returned ball, and head back to the alley.

Randomly, I pick a pin that I want knocked down. It's either one or the other, and since I can't beat Cole, I can try to beat the score I currently have. I've never been a bad sport. I'm not actually a sports person at all; I've never been good at it, but doing this with Cole makes me want to try other things that bring him joy just so I can see that joy on a regular basis.

I aim and roll.

Gutter.

"Fuck," I hiss, my balled-up fists snapping to my hips.

The laughter booms from behind me, and goose bumps rise over my skin at the sound of it. It's quickly becoming my favorite sound.

I can't help but giggle, turn, and head back to Cole. He stands and wraps me in a loser's embrace, and his chest vibrates against my cheek as he tries to rein it all back in.

When his laughter subsides, I tip my head back and rest my chin against his sternum. "Another round?"

Tenderly, he draws circles at the small of my back. Heat flickers in his eyes, and it's then that I know his mind has wandered somewhere else. "I have other ideas."

"Oh?"

He bends and whispers huskily in my ear, "And it doesn't involve the public eye."

A shiver starts from my head and ends at my toes. He lets me go, crouches before me, and starts to remove my rented bowling shoes. His face is so damn close to my core that I'm positive he's doing that to tease me. It's working. A tingle spreads from my clit to my nipples, a promise of what might come.

As soon as my shoes are off, he slides off his own, picks up our shoes, and passes them to me. "Return these? I'll put back the balls."

I nod, take them, and we each briefly head our separate ways. A hum works its way up my throat, a happy tune on my way to the counter. I set them down on the surface, and the person who's manning the shoes turns and does a double-take at me.

A smile spreads across his sickly-looking face. "Tegan," Derek greets hoarsely. It's as if he'd spent the majority of the night screaming at a rock concert and now has a raw throat.

"Mr. Wordon," I say in surprise, and then it hits me. He owns this bowling alley. Sort of. Well, he wouldn't at all if he knew about the living will.

"It's Derek," he corrects, his smile fading a little.

"Right. Sorry." I shift awkwardly, because the more the seconds tick by, the more he studies me.

"Did you come with your friend? Tori, right?" he asks, searching the space behind me.

I shake my head. "Cole and I came together."

He raises his eyebrows above the rim of his

glasses. Deep wrinkles stretch across his forehead, loose skin from all the weight he's lost. "Cole?"

I nod while frowning because I don't like his tone.

"I see. Did you two have a good time?" For some odd reason, he doesn't seem too happy that I'm here with his handyman. I have no idea why, and I don't care to ask. It's none of his business anyway.

"We did. But we're headed out now. I just came to return our shoes." I point at them to redirect his attention.

He only glances at them. After a small bout of coughs, he asks, "You two getting close?"

I shift uncomfortably. "Yeah, yeah, we are."

He nods after a moment's pause. "That explains why he knows what you found."

My brows pinch together. "I'm sorry?"

Splaying both hands on the counter, he leans toward me. "A folder or binder or something of my brother's. He said you found it."

I don't correct him and tell him that it was actually Cole who found it. Instead, the cheeseballs in my stomach roll with nervous energy. Do I lie? No. I can't lie. I won't make Cole out to be the bad guy. Cole may not know the significance of what I found because I haven't told him yet, but I certainly do.

So instead of denying it, because I've never been a big fat liar, I just nod.

His eyes narrow as he looks down at me. "I'd like for you to hand that over to me."

"Why?" is my immediate question.

"Because it belonged to my brother. Therefore, it belongs to me."

My scowl is deep. "I thought you wanted anything we found in the house to be thrown away."

He tips his chin in a scolding sort of way, but I don't cower as he says, "That binder probably has important information in it."

"Then it should go to your stepbrother."

His head tilts to the side. "Why?"

I cross my arms and prop my elbows on the counter. "Because the only important information you could possibly need from a dead guy is something that will help the cops in his murder."

His eyes narrow even further until they're little, accusatory slits. "Are you implying that I don't want to find my brother's killer?"

I shrug a little to hide the fact that I hadn't thought much about it until this very moment. In fact, I'm starting to see it much more clearly. Derek and Neil didn't get along. There's legal evidence of it. And the fact that Derek received absolutely nothing from his parents, nor would he receive anything from him in the will...*yeah*. Yeah, that's suspicious as hell. "If you don't want the binder turned over to the cops, then yes."

He leans a little more so that he's in my face. Again, I don't back down. I don't know why, but I'm a little protective over my ghost. I may have said that I don't want to find out what he wants, but as the days go by, it's obvious that he wants something. The question is: do I feel an obligation to him? I don't have an answer to that yet.

And then there's the matter of Cole's job and living situation.

"I assure you," he begins slowly, threateningly. "I want nothing more than to find my brother's murderer. I even have a reward out for it."

I scoff. I know by now that Derek is cheap. He hoards his money. The only reason he'd put an award out for his brother's killer is if he knew they'd never be found. Why else would he have a reward for evidence to find out what happened to a brother he hated? To a brother that was leaving him nothing if he happened to pass on?

Yeah, I see right through that.

"Well, you're not getting the binder. The binder will be turned in to the police."

His hand snatches out so fast that I gasp when his fingers wrap tightly around my upper arm. "You *will* give me the binder, Tegan," he hisses.

I try to yank my arm out of his grasp. "You're hurting me, Derek."

"What's going on?" a deep, familiar voice asks beside me. I glance over to find Cole glaring at Derek's hand. He raises his dark gaze to Derek, and, dare I say it, a little nervous flicker crosses Derek's face.

"She won't give me the binder," Derek explains defensively as he roughly removes his hand from my arm.

I rub at the skin that will surely have bruises. "If the cops want you to have it, they'll give it to you."

He opens his mouth to say something, but Cole holds up a hand. I don't peek at Cole to see what sort of look he's giving him, but whatever it is, it silences him in a second. "I don't ever want to see you touch her again." Cole's voice is deep and dangerous, and it sends a shiver over my body.

"I—she—" Derek stutters and points at me.

Cole leans a little into the counter. "No excuses. Lay another finger on her and I'll break it off."

"You can't threaten your landlord like that!"

"And how do you think the cops will take it when they find out you've threatened your tenant over what could possibly be evidence?" Cole asks so quietly that I barely hear him. It's then I realize that we're drawing attention, and if I don't wrap this up quickly, people will start to ask questions. He leans away from the counter, and a little more loudly, he adds, "I don't know why you want it, Derek, but you'll have to fight the cops for it."

Derek's face pales a smidge, making the dark circles under his eyes stand out. God, he looks horrible. Whatever illness he has is wasting him away. For a split second, I almost feel bad for him.

Cole gently takes my elbow and steers me away from the counter. I follow him without a fuss for a few reasons. One, because I know Cole is close to the breaking point and he needs me to be his rock in this moment. Two, because I want the hell out of here as much as he does. By now, everyone has stopped to stare at us. I can feel their eyes crawling all over my skin as we pass.

Instead of cowering under the weight of it, however, I remove my elbow from Cole's hand and twine my fingers with his. They can stare all they want. They can speculate, draw conclusions. It's Cole and me against the town, and I won't give them any reason to believe otherwise.

CHAPTER 19
COLE GARNER

Crickets sing as Tegan takes my hand while we stride up to her front door. She's only let go of it when necessary since we left the bowling alley. I know why, too. It doesn't take a genius to figure that out. She saw my true side, a small piece of me that I keep buried, and because of that, she has to know I'm on edge.

With her fingers between mine, it keeps my demons at bay. I saw Derek's hand grasping her forearm, the look on his face, and I almost lost it completely. For a second, my past had come back to haunt me. For a second, I became that seventeen-year-old boy.

But her hand. Her warmth. Her comfort. It reminded me that she was okay, that the situation was handled, and with her hand, I could breathe. It was the exorcism of my ghosts. I don't know if she knows how grateful I am for it, how much I don't actually deserve it, but how greedily I'll take it.

I open the door for us and flick on the lights as we step inside.

"Come with me," she murmurs. Her hand tightens against mine, and she leads us through the hall and into her bedroom. She keeps the lights off as she shuts the door, bathing us in deep shadows. Silently, she turns to me, lets go of my hand, and lifts my shirt over my head.

"What are you doing?" I ask when her lips pepper my bare chest.

She flings the shirt to the side and whispers against my skin, "Giving you what you need."

"And what do I need?" My voice is rumbling, half because I'm still on edge and half because her touching me like that is making my cock hard. This isn't the usual way we begin sex. No, this is something entirely different because the way she's kissing my body has meaning.

She rises onto her tiptoes and presses a soft and lingering peck to my mouth. "A reminder that someone cares about you." A small smile plays on her lips. "And a reminder that if you go back and stab Derek, you'll be missed when you're back in prison."

I grunt my response, but it's enough to satisfy her because she backs away and strips out of her shirt and bra.

"Take off your pants and shoes," she orders quietly after letting me visibly roam her tits while flexing my hands at my sides with the urge to touch her.

As she slides out of her own jeans and shoes, she heads to the bathroom and flicks on the light. The spray of the shower's water comes next, and reading her intent, I do as she asks. I strip, leave my clothes in a heap, and follow her into the bathroom.

My eyes roam her backside as she bends and prepares the shower, the way each curve slopes, the creamy pallor of her skin, the way her hair slides against her soft shoulders when she bends over. Even though her back is to me, she's just as beautiful from behind as she is from the front.

She turns a sly smile back at me before sliding the curtain aside and stepping into the tub. I don't have to be asked to follow her. As soon as I'm in, the warm water beats against my back and slides over my shoulders. She grabs her soap, gathers it in her hand, and starts lathering my chest.

"I can wash myself," I say quietly.

"Sure, sure," she answers distractedly. Her eyes are transfixed on my body, and I don't miss the extra attention that my abs get. They ripple under her touch, making my cock even harder. I've never been touched like this. Hell, I've never showered with a woman before. I have no idea how this is supposed to go, but Tegan seems content with leading this for now, so I let her.

She applies more soap to her hand and dips to the V of my thighs. I suck in a breath as she skates over my tight balls.

Grabbing her wrist, unable to not have her wrap her fingers around it, I guide her soapy hand to my cock. My head bows forward in pure fucking heaven when she doesn't fight me and wraps her fingers around it. I don't let go of her wrist as I direct her hand to slide up and down my shaft. I may have let her direct the beginning of this shower, but apparently, I'm incapable of letting her direct *this*.

Using her other hand, she cups my balls and gently kneads. A moan escapes me, and I raise my hand to grab the back of her neck and bring her closer to me. My lips are on her instantly, and she kisses me back while continuing to pleasure me with goddamn soap.

I lick the seam of her mouth, asking her to open for me, and at the same time, she grips me firmly. Pleasure shoots up my spine, and I groan as my tongue dives into her mouth. She returns to sliding her hand up and down my length, scraping her nails against my balls, and exploring my mouth with her tongue. Goose bumps cover my flesh, contracting my muscles and making me swell in her hand. But a part of me doesn't like that she's trying to direct this again, so I grab her neck and squeeze a little.

Her chuckle is a little strangled, but she pushes me back into the water and lets the spray wash away the soap. Curious, I release her mouth and take in her swollen lips and mischievous gaze.

Holding onto my hips, she crouches until she's on her knees. Her lips part, and knowing exactly what she's planning, my heart skips a beat. She grabs the base and flicks her tongue against my cock's tip. I jolt in surprise, and I brace one hand on the wall.

She smiles as I blow out a breath, preparing myself for what's to come. It's been years since I've had a woman's mouth around me. I don't even remember what it feels like, but my imagination runs wild, and aside from the warm water sliding down my back, my skin heats.

I exhale a groan when she runs her tongue from my balls to the tip and then breathe deep when she nibbles her way back down. And then she opens wide and slides my length inside. My next groan is deep, and my fingers curl against the shower wall. So fucking warm. So fucking wet. So fucking *mine.*

My other hand tangles in her slightly damp strands. Gently, I guide her deeper. She can't take me all the way down. In fact, I barely fit, but when her throat constricts in a gag, I rumble, "Fuck."

Tears gather in her eyes as I hold her there. It's a beautiful fucking sight, her choking on me.

I curse under my breath as I finally release her. She takes a moment to suck in air, but like the sweetheart she is, she doesn't wipe away the tears that are smearing her makeup. When she has her breathing under control, I guide her back to me, controlling the rhythm with my hand still in her hair.

She pumps her other hand along my base to make up for what her mouth can't fit, and together, her wet, slightly cold hand and her warm, soaked mouth make the muscles in my legs tighten.

I curl and uncurl my hand against the shower wall, fighting for something to grab onto as intense pleasure takes over. And then she hollows out her mouth, sucking me in. A hiss escapes me, and my hand tightens in her hair to the point that it must be painful. But instead of complaining of pain, she groans, and it vibrates against me.

"Fuck," I curse again, this time a little louder.

Her hollowed-out cheeks, the saliva dripping from her chin, and her watery eyes looking up at me in lust...it's a fucking wet dream.

"That's it, sweetheart," I rumble. "Suck in a breath."

She does as I ask, and when I'm satisfied that she has enough air, I grip her head with both hands and fucking use her. My hips thrust forward, and I fuck her mouth like it's mine to do what I please. Her hands fly to my thighs to steady herself, and every now and then —every few pumps—she gags.

I moan as a tingle travels down my spine and settles into my balls. Her nails rake my thighs, and it sends me over the edge. Growling, I pull out, grab my base, and pump. "Open," I demand.

She does, sticking her tongue out to catch every last drop of cum that spills out of my cock. I moan as I make a mess of her face, as I take every ounce of pleasure of her on her knees, mouth open and a needy, desperate look to taste every bit of me.

When I'm finished, she leans and licks the tip, gathering the bead that was left there. After she swallows, I take her hands and help her stand. Cum drips from the edges of her lips and slides down the edges of her cheeks.

"So fucking beautiful," I murmur to her.

A blush rises to her cheeks, a stark contrast to the cum, but I move so I can guide her into the spray. Once the cum is washed off, I turn her back to me and kiss her tenderly. "Thank you," I say against her mouth.

She looks back at me and juts her chin in surprise.

"What?" I ask, concerned.

"I never thought I'd ever hear you thank anyone."

I don't know how to tell her how grateful I am, so I just shrug. She brought me back from the edge, and even though I still have concerns and issues, she took the time to distract me, to give me what I needed even when I didn't know what I needed: *her*.

She gave me her.

I kiss her forehead as I pick up her soap. I quickly wash her and then myself, both of us lost in thought. The night is coming to a close, and even I have to admit that I don't want it to be over.

Turning off the shower, she slides back the curtain and plucks two towels from the rack. We dry off, sneaking a few kisses in between, and step out of the shower. In the dark room, I head to my clothes, and just as I pick up my shirt, she says, "No."

I turn and raise an eyebrow. "No?"

She shakes her head. "Will you , um—" She looks at the bed, then back at me, nibbling her lip.

"Stay with you?" I finish for her.

She nods. "At least until I fall asleep."

I drop my shirt back to the ground, head to the bed, and climb in. Truth be told, I don't want to leave either. I do have a lot to think about—about the evening at the bowling alley, about the way she brought me back from the edge, about all of it—but there's no way I can deny her this. *Deny* me *this*. I can think about the rest of the shit when I head home.

Smiling, she crosses the room and slides under the

covers with me. Her body curls against mine, and she exhales contentedly when I drape my arm around her.

I kiss the top of her damp hair. I may not deserve this, and I may only be staying until sleep takes her, but like hell am I going to give it up.

Call me selfish, and I won't deny it.

CHAPTER 20
TEGAN ADAMS

My eyes fly open when I hear someone say, "Wake up." It was screamed right in my ear from a deep male voice. I startle and scramble with the covers, fighting for breath that just won't come. It takes me a moment to realize I'm in my room, and it takes me even longer, eyes wildly searching the darkness, to realize that I'm alone.

Even Cole is gone.

I work on calming my breathing, long passes between O-shaped lips, as I come to grips with the fact that the scream was probably in my dream. I don't remember what I was dreaming about, but it had to have been a bad one to wake up in such a way.

And the ringing in my ears? That's blood rushing through them. That's all.

I'm sure Dr. Lynn would have had something to say about all this, but in this moment, I can't think of one piece of advice he'd give me.

I stretch my arm out across the mattress and feel

that Cole's side of the bed is cold. He's been gone for a while, and I find myself a little disappointed that he didn't stay. But he had something happen to him last night that I know he needs to think about, so I try to be understanding and let that wash away my disappointment.

The covers drape down my bare torso as I work myself into a sitting position. My heart still hammers, and a fine sweat has broken across my back, but sitting will help me come to grips with reality.

I stick a finger in my ear and wiggle, trying to get the hearing back to normal. And then I sit there for a moment, waiting for my heart to calm, before I climb out of the bed, throw on a big T-shirt, and head into the bathroom. The water splutters as I turn it on, but I cup my hands under the faucet and splash the cold water on my face. I have no idea what time it is, but based on how dark it still is, it has to be the middle of the night.

As I pat my face dry, I stare at my exhausted expression in the mirror. The color is drained from my cheeks, but I sort of expected that after that scare.

Sighing, I decide to keep the bathroom light on because, for some odd reason, a little light makes me feel a smidge safer. My mother used to leave the hall light on to chase away the bad dreams, so the bathroom light should work just the same. In theory, anyway.

I head back to my bedroom, the light splashing across the bed. I almost didn't see it. In my exhausted state, and if it were dark in my room, I would have missed it entirely until morning.

There, across my bed, are at least a dozen rose petals.

A chill dribbles down my spine, and I suck in a fast breath as I take a step toward my bed on numb feet. Were they there when I woke up? Did I not see them in the dark? Or...

On instinct, I slowly turn my head toward the cheval mirror. The pasture is in full view under the moonlight, and there, walking toward the patch of roses, is a man. With bated breath, I watch him. His hands are stuffed into his pockets, and his shoulders are slightly slumped, but even from the side profile, and even though he's transparent, I know who that is.

Neil Wordon.

When he makes it to the rose patch, he pauses. And then he turns and looks directly at my window.

My heart skips a beat, and my hand flies to my mouth. Fresh tears prick my eyes, because, even though I'm watching him through a mirror, I know he sees me. I know he knows I'm watching him. And I know he wants my attention.

Stupidly, and without meaning to, I take a step toward the window that the mirror is reflecting. My whole body shakes as I do, but I have to see for myself. I have to know, without a mirror.

I take another step.

And then another, until I'm standing right before it with my eyes squeezed shut.

"Come on, Tegan," I whisper to myself, punctuating it with a sob.

Swallowing thickly, I pry my eyes open.

And then I scream and scramble back because,

right there, just outside my window, Neil stands. His eyes are pinned on mine, and he has a serious expression on his face.

My entire nervous system screams until my limbs are almost painful, but I can't take my eyes off of him. They're stuck open, my brain unable to comprehend this see-through man just outside my window.

He lifts his closed fist to the height of his shoulder, and I watch with absolutely crippling fear as he opens his fingers one by one. Petals drift from his palm and float away in the breeze.

I scream again, but he doesn't move. His eyes are trained on mine.

"What do you want?" I yell.

Again, he only watches me.

My breath heaves, and I swear to God there isn't enough oxygen in this room. Every instinct in me is telling me to jump into the bed and cover my head with the blankets. To run away. To go back to Chicago, where ghosts don't haunt me.

"What do you want?" I ask again, gripping my hair on both sides of my head.

Slowly, he turns his head toward the pasture.

"Why are you haunting me?" I demand. My body racks with sobs, my heart slamming against my ribs. My roots scream as I tug my hair even harder.

When he looks back at me, I fight through the tears blurring my vision. "Why? What do you want from me? Please. Please go away. *Please!"*

His expression remains blank, but I clearly see him looking toward my dresser. Even though I'm scared to, I look with him. Sitting on top of my dresser is my tote with the binder tucked inside, exactly where I left it. I swallow, but my mouth is completely dry.

The binder? What does he want with the binder?

I turn to demand an answer to my question, but he's walking away, back toward the pasture. I stand there for a moment, wondering if I'm crazy, if everything that just happened is a dream. But as I wipe away the tears streaming down my face, I realize how real this is. My hands come away wet, and the chill of the room wraps around my body, all evidence that this is truly reality.

On their own accord, my feet start moving toward the window again. I peer through it, and there he is, walking toward the pasture. He walks right through the fence, and as soon as he reaches the roses, he looks back at me once before he fades away.

I hiccup and let out another sob.

This is real. *That* was real.

With a sudden urgency, I rush to my phone, yank it off the charger, and unlock the screen. My fingers pause against the screen. I can't call the cops. They wouldn't believe me, and if I did, they'd demand the binder. Besides, what can they possibly do against a ghost?

I can't call Derek. He wouldn't believe me any more than the cops, and he'd just demand the binder again. I could call Cole, but I don't want to bother him, and he doesn't know the full story yet. He only knows the beginning of the haunting, and we haven't talked about it since.

Decision made, I pull up Tori's contact and bring it

to my ear. It rings almost until the voicemail answers, but she picks up, and her groggy voice comes through.

"Tegan, it's the middle of the fucking night."

"Tori!" I nearly shout, dashing back to the window, but he's not there. There's no evidence that he was, except for the rose petals drifting away across the grass.

"What?"

"He was here," I whisper feverishly.

"Who?"

"Neil Wordon." I rake a hand through my hair. "Oh god, I'm going crazy. That's what this is. He knows I'm crazy, so he's haunting me. He knows I'm afraid of death, so he's playing with me."

"Slow down," she coos. She pauses, and I can hear a light being flicked on through the phone. "Tell me what happened."

"Neil!" I growl loudly. "He was at my window!"

"Just…wait. What?"

I nod like she can see me and step away from the window to pace the room. The light from the bathroom makes the corners of the room cast deep shadows. I glance wildly at them, terrified that Neil will be waiting in them. "He left rose petals on my bed and then he was in my mirror and then he was by the roses and then he was at my window."

"And you saw him? Are you sure?" There's no disbelief in her voice, but I'm talking so fast that I know she's trying to break it down.

"Yes! He brought petals with him. They're still on the ground. I didn't make this up, Tori. I swear to God."

She shushes me like a child. "I know. I believe you."

I breathe a sigh of relief and plop down on the edge of my bed.

"Do you, ah, what did he want?"

I lift my head to the tote. "He looked at the binder."

"The one you brought to work?"

"Yeah," I whisper.

"Well," she begins, blowing out a breath. "Whatever he wants from you has to do with that binder, Tegan."

I flex my jaw as I stand from the bed and head to the dresser. Carefully, as though it's made of glass, I slide the binder out. "You really think I should entertain him, and what? Discover what he wants from the binder so that he can move on?"

"Yeah," she says. "Yeah, I think you should."

As I head back to my bed with the binder, I murmur, "I should just turn this in."

"Not until you help him move on. Otherwise, he's going to continue to haunt you."

"Right," I whisper. "My therapist would be having a field day with this."

She's quiet for a moment. "The whole afraid of death thing?" she asks quietly.

"Well, yeah. I mean, he'd think my brain was making this up to deal with my fear."

"Probably," she says. "But he'd be wrong. Do you want me to come over so we can look together?"

I know she's asking if I don't want to be alone. But truth be told, and although it was scary at the time, I'm not as scared as I should be. "No, I'll be fine," I breathe. "I promise. I'm just going to go through this, and I'll report back to you tomorrow."

"Okay." Her tone is unsure, but she doesn't fight me on it. "Call me back in the morning, okay, babe?"

I nod. "Talk to you soon."

As soon as I hang up, I open the binder and flip through the pages that I've already looked at. I may not have wanted to help Neil before, but I do now, because I know if I don't, he'll never leave me alone. For some reason, and perhaps it's because I live here, he's chosen me. I don't know if that makes me stupid or smart, but I'm trying not to think about it at all.

CHAPTER 21
COLE GARNER

I frown as I pull up to Tegan's house. The sun is barely up, but every single light in the house is on. Normally, it's just her bedroom light that splashes across the grass at dawn. Normally, she doesn't venture out into the house until I get there. I cringe a little, hoping like hell she isn't awake and at it this morning because she's pissed that I left.

Honestly, I didn't want to leave once she fell asleep, but I knew I was no good to her the way I was. I needed to clear my head, so I visited my sister's grave and sat against her stone for a while. When my ass became numb, I kissed the stone, left, and headed back to my trailer. I sat on my couch for a while, thinking about everything. Trying to sort my thoughts and categorize these fresh and new feelings I was having. Eventually, I got sick of myself and worked out until my limbs were shaking. But I couldn't stay away from her long, and even though I didn't get a wink of sleep, I showered, dressed, and headed back out.

I had to see her again. I was compelled to.

Donuts was a spur-of-the-moment decision. I wasn't surprised that the owner of the shop knew that I was picking up Tegan's as well. Word of Tegan and me together had spread fast, but thankfully, she didn't say anything on the subject. She just passed me the donuts and waved me away to take the next order.

Parking my truck, I snatch the bag of donuts from the passenger side and get out of the cab. I head to the house, a little worried about what I'll walk in on. This is all new for me. I don't know what is acceptable behavior and what isn't. But she knows that, doesn't she? She knows this is foreign for me, right?

There's only one way to find out.

I pull the door open and step inside. Immediately, I smell coffee, and I follow my nose through the living room. "Tegan?" I call.

"In here," she says from the kitchen.

As I enter the kitchen, I hold up the bag of donuts, but Tegan doesn't even look up at me. She's poring over the binder, almost pretending that I don't exist.

Shit.

"You're mad," I state, gently setting the donuts by her elbow.

"Huh?" She glances up at me distractedly.

I raise my eyebrows. "About me leaving in the middle of the night?"

Her expression relaxes, and she waves a hand in the air. "No, no, not at all. Coffee is over there." She flicks her thumb behind her to the full coffee pot.

I step farther into the kitchen, a little confused, and head to the empty mug set out for me. As I pour myself a generous amount, I scowl at the steam. "Why are you up already?"

Turning, I see her shoulders bunch before she swivels toward me with a guilty expression. "I, uh, something happened last night."

"After I left?" I ask. Did Derek come? Did he demand the binder in the middle of the night? He would do something like that, I wouldn't put it past him, especially after our encounter at the bowling alley. "Was it Derek?"

"No, no," she answers, crossing her arms over her chest uncomfortably. "His brother."

"Smith?" I cock my head to the side. What would the sheriff be doing out here in the middle of the night?

She shakes her head. "Neil."

My eyes narrow. "I don't follow."

The way she talks next, fast and full of stutters, causes me to set my mug down. The wild direction of her spewing is like whiplash, and it takes a moment for me to register everything she says.

"His ghost? Neil Wordon's ghost?" I ask, making sure I have all the facts.

She nods. I look at the binder laid open behind her, and my brows pinch together.

"Do you think I'm crazy?" she asks when I don't say anything for several seconds.

I shake my head. "No. I believe you. It's, uh, just strange."

Her shoulders sag with relief. "Good, because

otherwise, I'd show you the rose petals all over my bed."

"On your bed?" I repeat.

She nods again. "I haven't cleaned them up yet. Do you want to see them?"

My skin rises in goose bumps because she has direct evidence that something did happen here. Instead of answering her though, because I'm not sure I want anything to do with a ghost other than those of my past, I grab my mug and step toward her and the binder. "Did you find what he wanted?"

Her expression brightens, and she turns back toward the binder. She grabs a packet of papers held together by a paperclip. "This."

"What is it?"

"Emails," she whispers. "Between Derek and Neil."

"What are they about?"

She blows out a breath and leafs through the papers. "They're mostly copies of what Derek sent Neil. They're all threats, though."

"What kind of threats?" I ask as I lean forward to catch a few words.

"Death threats."

I raise my gaze to hers. "Why?" After last night, I'm not surprised that Derek would threaten his brother, but the question is, why would he feel the need to?

She shrugs a little. "He wanted on the living will." She drops the packet back into the binder and crosses her arms back over her chest. "He did it, Cole."

Picking back up my coffee, I lift the mug to my lips, humoring her. "He did what?"

The paper crinkles as she jabs it with a finger. "He killed Neil." I give her a look of disbelief, so she prattles on. "The emails, death threats, restraining order...I mean, come on, Derek has a reward to find his killer."

"You think Derek put out the reward, knowing it would never be cashed out?"

She nods vigorously. "You said yourself that he's a cheap man."

I consider this for a moment. By rights, it would be a good story if he promised a reward to get suspicion off his back. Nobody suspected him to begin with, but maybe that's the reason why. He was willing to put up a shit ton of money...

"What do you think?" she asks quietly. "Do you believe me?"

I prop a hip on the counter. "It's possible. But there's nothing you can do about it until you call the cops and turn this over. They'll definitely look into it."

A small smile pulls at the corners of her lips as she says, "I already did. The sheriff should be here any minute."

My nostrils flare. I don't want anything to do with Smith, but it would make sense why he'd take the call. "You didn't tell him about the ghost, did you?"

She scowls. "I'm not stupid. He thinks his brother is still alive."

"He may not after what he finds in the binder."

"Yeah," she says, sighing. "I hate to be the one who hands him the evidence that Neil is dead. I mean, he *is* dead, but it's going to break Sheriff Smith's heart."

"There's nothing you can do about that," I add, reaching and shutting the binder.

She zips it up and steps toward me, curling her body against mine. I set the mug back down and kiss the top of her head while wrapping my arms around her waist. We stand there like that, both of us thinking over the possibilities of what Tegan discovered, all the way up until a knock sounds at the door.

She pulls away and picks up the binder. "That'll be him."

I follow her out of the kitchen, through the dining room, and to the front door. She opens it with the binder tucked into the crook of her arm. By now, the sun is fully risen, and the reflection of it shines glaringly against Smith's black hat.

Smith smiles brightly at Tegan, but then his smile fades when he sees me. "Morning," he says.

"Thank you for coming," Tegan greets, stepping outside. She makes room for me to come out with her, and I shut the door behind us.

"How's the house coming along?" he asks, making an attempt at small talk while trying to discreetly shoot daggers at me with his eyes. Probably, in his tiny mind, he thinks I spent the night. I smirk back at him, letting him think that his assumption is right, even if it isn't.

"Oh, um—" Tegan looks back at the house. "It's coming along."

"Good," he says, bobbing his head. Slapping his

thigh, he adds, "So, I heard you have something for me."

"Right," Tegan answers. She holds out the binder for him to take. "We found this. It's legal information of Neil's."

He gently takes the binder. "In the house?"

"Yeah." A guilty expression takes over Tegan's face, and she pulls at her fingers nervously.

He weighs the binder in his hand as he looks at her suspiciously. "Did you look in it?"

She cringes, and I have the urge to escort this asshole back to his car. I don't like his tone. "I may have. But not all of it. Just some of it."

He raises an eyebrow at her. "And what did you find?"

Blowing out a breath, she looks at me for a second. I nod, urging her on. "Evidence that your stepbrother killed Neil."

His eyes widen in shock. "Neil isn't dead, Tegan."

"I'm sorry," she whispers. "But there's just too much evidence that he is."

"Then where is the body?" he asks.

She fidgets a little. "I don't know any of that information."

"Then you don't know he's dead, but you took it upon yourself to play detective anyway?"

I grind my teeth. "Just look at the evidence, Smith."

He points at me. "You're the last person who should be looking into any murder."

We stand there for a moment, glaring at each other,

until Tegan breaks the silence. "Will you please just look at what we found?"

His curt nod only pisses me off further. The lack of respect for her shouldn't surprise me, but color me surprised anyway. She's passing him evidence of what could close his stepbrother's case, and he's being an asshole about it because it might tell him how dead he really is. "I'll take it in and have a look."

"Thank you," she breathes out.

"Tegan, if you don't mind, I'd like to talk to Cole alone."

My eyebrows raise, and though she looks at me for confirmation, I keep my focus solely on Smith.

"Sure," she eventually says.

As soon as she's back inside, Smith takes a threatening step in my direction, which is humorous because he's shorter than I am. I get some satisfaction that he has to look up at me as he growls, "I don't want you anywhere near her." He shakes the binder between us. "You put these ideas in her head, didn't you?"

I raise an eyebrow. "She came to these conclusions all on her own."

He chuffs. "And I'm supposed to believe the word of a killer?"

I only shrug, which turns his face a perfect shade of red.

"I hear the rumors, Garner. I know you two are together, and I'm warning you to stay away."

"Because my happiness would only serve to piss you off? If you ask me, that's an incentive to do the opposite."

He raises a hand to jab me in the chest with a

finger but thinks better of it, closes it into a fist, and drops it down to his side. "Does she know about your past?"

I nod. "She does."

"Then you didn't tell her the full truth."

I laugh quietly. "Oh, I did. She knows everything."

His eyes narrow. "Then she's a fool."

I flex my jaw. "Why don't you go back to the pigpen and look into what she gave you?"

"Yeah," he nearly growls. "I'll do that."

He turns on his booted heel and strides back to his car. More like waddles. While his stepbrother loses the weight, he seems to be gaining it.

"Smith," I bark. He pauses in his step. "Don't bury this like you bury everything else."

Without looking back at me, he raises a hand over his head and gives me the middle finger. I get a little satisfaction out of that too because I'm not a little boy anymore. He can't sweep it under the rug or hide it from the light. He knows I'll come after him if he does, consequences be damned, because, like last time, I won't let someone I care about be hurt. Not in any way.

CHAPTER 22

TEGAN ADAMS

I try like hell not to bite my nails as I wait for Cole to come back inside. This is it. I could have solved a murder. Time will tell, I suppose, because Sheriff Smith is right. I'm not a detective, but I know that they'll look into it. Even the sheriff can't deny the mounting evidence against Derek. The only problem is, if he's caught red-handed, I don't know what happens to me. To Cole. I could have doomed us both, but honestly, I had no choice.

I won't let Neil's death be in total vain because I don't want my boyfriend to lose his job, his house, and his basic livelihood. What kind of person would that make me? One I wouldn't like.

The door opens, and Cole steps through. His expression is blank, and I pull at my fingers until the door shuts behind him. "What did he want?"

Cole shakes his head a little, but I note the tiniest bit of humor on his face. I frown at it as he says, "He told me to stay away from you."

He travels around the couch and takes a seat. I follow him, slowly sitting down directly beside him. "What? Why?"

The small smile is still there when he turns his head to look me in the eyes. "He thinks I'm corrupting you. That I'm putting these ideas in your head about his dead brother."

My frown deepens. "You aren't corrupting me."

Raising his arm, he rests it against the back of the couch and toys with the ends of my hair. "I know."

I lean my head back a little, enjoying the feeling of my hair being played with. My eyelids flutter when his hand moves to my scalp and massages the roots of my hair. "What else was said?"

He leans and tugs the shoulder of my shirt to bare my shoulder. Gently, he presses a kiss and murmurs against my skin, "I told him not to bury the evidence like he did for my sister."

A small sigh escapes me as he moves further up my shoulder. "Sometime, I'd like to meet your sister."

He freezes for a moment before moving to my neck. I tip my head to the side, and as soon as he nips, my nipples pebble. "She's dead. You can't meet her."

"I have proof that there is life beyond the grave," I breathe out. What he's doing to me is lighting me on fire. My entire body is hyper-aware of every single little touch.

"Mmm," he hums against my skin.

"She'd know we were there," I whisper while his lips brush against my jaw.

"Mmm," he hums again. "Sweetheart?"

Instantly, I'm aware and alert because every time

he uses that nickname, I usually come shortly after. "What?"

"Lie down," he orders softly into my ear.

Topic forgotten, I do as he says, using the armrest of the couch to prop my head. The couch bounces a little as he shifts, hooks his fingers under my shorts, and slides them down in such a sensual way that goose bumps rise across my thighs.

"Take your shirt off," he orders again, but this time, his voice is deep and husky, and damn it if it doesn't do something to me.

He drops my shorts and underwear beside the couch as I lift myself up a little, taking off my shirt and bra and gently setting them on the ground.

Naked before him, the chill of the room caresses my skin while his eyes rake over my body. Heat flashes in his gaze before it settles on my face. My clit throbs at the attention, at the way he's looking at me from the other end of the couch.

He lifts a leg onto the cushion in a bent position to better angle his body, and then his hands slide up my ankles, over my knees, and down my thighs. I shiver when the rough skin of his fingers brushes against my throbbing clit while his other hand pushes my knees further apart, baring myself to him. I don't know if he's even aware that he's doing it, but his tongue darts out to lick the corner of his lips like he's imagining what I taste like. But there's no room for us on this couch for him to put his lips on my pussy, and he seems to know that because, instead, he slides a finger through my slit and carefully pushes it inside me.

I moan at the intrusion as he murmurs, "So wet, sweetheart."

He pulls out his finger, and a protest rests on my lips, but whatever I was going to say quickly flees. An expert, drenched finger starts to circle my clit. My thighs quiver around his arms, but he keeps them apart. A silent order. A demand. A promise that he'll let me come as long as I do what I'm told.

Lifting myself slightly, I get a good look at what he's doing to me. The sight of him playing with my clit in slow, small strokes nearly has me coming undone.

Unable to help myself, I skate a hand over my breast and pinch my nipple. My head tips back, bumping the armrest as I moan.

The hand that was holding my thigh apart moves up my stomach and slides under my hand. He gently pulls my fingers off my nipple and replaces them with his own. The way his fingers tweak, flick, and pull shoots electric shocks straight to my pussy.

"Oh my god," I say as my eyelids flutter for a moment before I return to watch what he's doing to me.

The way he's transfixed on my pussy, the way my body reacts to what he's doing to me is the stuff an ordinary girl would dream about. It's like he can't get enough until he gets what he wants—me coming all over his fingers. And even then, I don't think that'll be enough for him. The way his cock strains against his jeans tells me otherwise.

He gathers himself on his knee and leans over me, his finger never leaving my clit, never deterring from his mission. The hand that was playing with my nipple skims along my collarbone until his fingers are circling my throat. He constricts my airway just enough to make it a little hard to breathe, and the blood to be semi-trapped in my face. And then he bends his head forward and sucks my nipple into his mouth.

My back arches off the couch, pushing my breast into his face, and I moan his name. The muscles in my thighs quiver around his hips, but he doesn't stop. His finger flicks at the same time as his tongue against my nipple, and it takes everything I have to not writhe against him. Not that he'd complain about that, but he'd stop what he's doing, and I can't have that. Not when I'm so close. Not when the fire is burning in my belly, waiting to release an orgasm from hell.

Head whipping back and forth, barely able to contain how lit my body is, how attuned it is to everything he's doing, my mewls and moans are strangled against his hand. My hips start to buck, and with one hum against my breast, I shatter.

I'm positive that if I had neighbors, they'd hear my scream. Everything—my pussy, my body, even my thoughts—constricts and explodes in a wave of pure, utter bliss. For a moment, I see little green stars in my vision, but he rides me out, waiting until the last drop of cum seeps out of me.

My body slacks against the couch, and I really fight for air against his hand. He releases my neck, letting me take in a much-needed breath, while he unbuttons his jeans. The way he pushes down his jeans isn't hurried. It isn't slow. It's confident and sure.

Saliva pools in my mouth, and my pussy clenches at the sight of his cock once it springs free. With one hand resting against the armrest of the couch, right by my head, he slides an arm underneath me and raises me to his cock's level. It's a complete fucking turn-on, the way his muscles bunch in his arm as he lifts me. I know I'm no small girl, and to have a man who can handle me...

He notches himself at my entrance and watches my pussy swallow him whole as he pushes inside. I suck in a sharp breath at the familiar sting of my walls stretching for him. At the same time, he groans, his fingers digging into the fabric of the armrest. He pulls my hips up higher, pushing even deeper inside me until I feel so damn full that my thoughts completely flee from my mind and my mouth falls wide open.

And then he's moving, pulling in and out with a lazy ease. Needing to feel him, I slip my hands under his shirt and grip the muscles of his back. They contract under my hands as he pumps into me. I hang on tight as he picks up his pace, our groans matching as his cock rubs just the right place. The sounds of our pleasure, of our bodies joining, fill the room, and together, we watch as his cock disappears and reappears from inside me. The stretch, the pressure against my G-spot...it's almost too much.

He glances up at me from under long lashes and growls, "Come for me, sweetheart. All over me."

My breathing picks up pace as the command he gives me only heightens my arousal. On their own accord, my hips start thrusting, meeting him every time he pushes inside. I start chasing that second orgasm, and at this point, my entire body is covered in a fine sheen of sweat. The heat coursing through my veins is intense, so intense that it matches the flames in my lower abdomen, waiting to be released.

He grits his teeth, and I know that he's as close as I am. The hand against the couch moves and collars me. He puts some weight into it, and every instinct in me tells me to fight back, but I don't because, even though I have instincts, it gives me intense pleasure to know that, yet again, my life is in his hands. The hands of someone who has killed before. The hands that belong to a man that I know would die before he saw anything bad happen to me.

And knowing this, knowing I'm at his mercy—my pussy, my pleasure, my life—I open my mouth to scream as my orgasm nearly breaks me in two.

"Fuck," he barks out. He picks up his pace, sliding faster in and out of me as my pussy clenches tightly around him. My vision starts to blacken, but, like all the other times, he seems to know and releases me.

I ride the rest of my orgasm while he grabs both of my hips and pounds into me, groaning and finding his own release. His head tips back as he pumps his cum into me, his cock twitching.

We come down from our high at the same time and meet each other's gaze while our chests heave for breath. He takes me in—my face, my hair, my neck—and smiles a little. "Fucking beautiful," he murmurs.

I'll never get sick of his displays of affection. For some odd reason, it means more coming from him than any other person I've met or dated before.

I gasp as he slowly pulls out of me. Cum starts to

dribble down, but he's quick in grabbing my shirt from the floor and cleaning me up. When he's done, he helps me back into my shorts and then lifts his ass to yank his jeans back up.

"I think we've fucked on every surface of this house," I say, a giggle punctuating it.

He smirks and lifts his gaze to the dining room. "Not the table."

I hold up a finger. "Stay away from that table. It's an antique."

As I sit up, he brings my head to his by gripping the back of my neck, and he kisses me. "So no sex on it?"

I shake my head as I stand up. "Absolutely not."

"Where are you going?" he asks as he watches me travel around the couch.

Looking over my shoulder, I answer, "To get a shirt."

His eyes skate my bare torso, and it gives me a thrill as I disappear down the hall and to my bedroom, riding that high from my orgasm and the fact that someone like me can turn him on so easily.

As soon as I open the door to my bedroom, my smile disappears. The breath I just gained back whooshes from my lungs as if I'd been punched. What is this? What in the hell is going on?

All over my bed, littered among the petals, are roses. Actual roses. A shiver runs down my spine, and it has nothing to do with my previous pleasure.

"Oh my god," I say, a hand flying to my mouth to cover my shock. "Cole!"

"What?" I hear him say calmly, but the way his

209

footsteps thunder through the house tells me he heard the urgency in my voice.

He comes down the hall and takes in my stiff stance, my terror. Looking into the room, he whispers, "What the fuck?"

"Did you do this?" I ask, prying my hand away from my face a little.

"No," he rumbles.

We stand there for a moment, staring at the mess of roses, before he moves past me and heads into the room. He picks up a rose and examines the stem. "They've been snapped."

"Snapped?" I repeat.

His gaze meets mine, and it's then he knows that I was telling him the truth, but just in case he wasn't sure, I whisper, "It's him. It's Neil."

His lips twist to the side for a moment before he carefully sets the rose back on my bed. "What does it mean?" he asks quietly.

I raise my gaze to the window, quickly throw on a shirt, and dash to it. My attention immediately goes to the mess of roses trapped by the barbed wire, but he isn't there. He's always there, in the dark, waiting while surrounded by . . .

And it's then that it hits me. "Oh my god," I whisper on an exhale.

"What?"

"The bed of roses…" My voice trails off.

He starts to make his way toward me, but I spin so fast that he stops. "His body. I mean, he's always by it. The petals, and now the roses. Cole!"

"What?" he asks, frowning.

I head to him quickly and grip his elbow. "He's buried under the roses."

His frown flattens, and he looks out the window as if he needs evidence for himself. He won't find any but their gentle sway in the breeze within their messy, trapped confines. "You know this for sure?"

I nod and squeeze his elbow. "I do." I start to move past him. "Come on, I'll show you."

He follows me quickly out of the room. "You're going to destroy that garden to find his body?"

I nod again as I head through the living room. My steps are determined because I know I'm right. It's what he's been trying to tell me, and now that I caught his brother, have evidence against him, he wants me to find the last piece: His bones. "Do you have a shovel?"

"No, but I have one in the trailer."

Swiveling, I turn and walk backward. "Go get it. I know he's buried there, Cole. He's been trying to tell me this entire time. Derek killed him and buried him there, then planted roses on top, fencing it off with barbed wire so the horses couldn't uproot the evidence."

"Why roses?"

I cock my head to the side as adrenaline starts to pump through my system. I know, without a doubt, that I'm right about this. "Because they were his step-mother's favorite. Who would question that sort of gardening when it was in her name that he did it?" For crying out loud, there are roses dedicated to her throughout the entire town.

Reaching the back door, I place my hand on the

doorknob as he says, "I won't be long. Give me about ten minutes."

I say nothing as I open the door and step out into the morning chill. The sound of his jogging through the house to get to the front door is cut off as soon as the door closes behind me, replaced by the sound of birds singing in the pasture's trees. As I stride across the uncut lawn to the fence, his truck's engine roars to life, and shortly after, I hear the tires crunch on the gravel as he drives away, leaving me alone on the property.

But I don't care about being alone. Not even knowing that Neil is here with me.

Carefully, I slide through a couple of posts holding up the fence and march straight for the roses. Once I'm there, I stand and examine the barbed wire. It's held together by posts that are already digging themselves out of the ground, thanks to the weight of the roses pressing against them.

With that in mind, I grab a post and yank with everything I have. It takes a few tries, but eventually, it's freed from the dirt. I throw the post as hard as I can over the bed of roses and stare at my next problem. *Thorns.*

Carefully, I start tugging the roots of the roses. Because of my firm grip, the thorns start to tear into my palms, but I barely notice it. The adrenaline is too great to feel much pain.

It has to have taken me a few minutes, but eventually, I've removed enough roses for enough dirt to be exposed. I drop to my knees and start digging with my cut-up hands. Cole will probably be pissed about that, but I have to know. I have to know if I'm right. It compels me, and I—

My fingers hit something hard. I freeze for a second before I start digging faster, whispering, "Oh my god," on repeat until what's fully revealed before me has a scream bubbling up in my chest.

There, covered in layers of dirt, is a skull.

"You just couldn't leave well enough alone, could you?" a familiar male voice says from behind me. It's punctuated with the sound of a gun being cocked.

CHAPTER 23
TEGAN ADAMS

"We shouldn't fear death, Tegan. It's the natural way of life," Dr. Lynn advised. "Someday, I'll die. Someday, you will too."

"And what about how you die, Dr. Lynn? Doesn't that scare you?"

He shrugs. "All we can do is hope that it's quick, and that, in itself, should put your mind at ease."

"Well, it doesn't."

The cock of the gun. That's all it takes for my blood to feel like ice. A split second and my greatest fear comes screaming back to life.

Slowly, I raise my hands and swivel to see the man I hadn't suspected.

Sheriff Smith's eyes are narrowed into slits, and although the majority of his face is pale, his cheeks are red. *Rage,* I realize. He must not have actually left the property; there are plenty of places to hide here. Or if he had, he stuck close by. And seeing Cole race away from it, he had to have known something was up.

"It was you," I whisper in shock, eyeing the barrel of the shotgun.

"Didn't count on that, did ya?" he huffs.

I gulp and shake my head. "Why?"

"Does it matter?" he growls.

My mouth runs dry as his grip on the gun tightens. I guess it doesn't matter. I'll die anyway, and his confession will end with me. But I have to know. I need to know. I need to see this through—for Neil.

"What did Neil ever do to you?" I manage to ask. My voice is cracked, shaking, as tears start to prick my eyes. The immediate problem of my death is near crippling, and on their own, my raised hands begin to shake.

"Everything!" he screams. In a nearby tree, birds take flight.

"Sheriff—" I say as I rise to my feet. Maybe, just maybe, I can talk him out of this. He's a man of the law, he should want to protect it.

And then I remember that he's not a man of the law. He killed his stepbrother. He hid his cousin's rape of an innocent little girl. This isn't a man of honor. He's a coward. And that thought settles in my gut because I'll be another check off his list of crimes.

"I was supposed to be the only one on his list."

The gun shakes as he tries to use hand gestures, but I say, "The will?" as I put two and two together.

"Yes," he hisses. "But then he grew a heart for his bastard brother. All the threats. All the trouble, and he

215

was going to put him in the will. Something about his father's wishes. Ridiculous, don't you think?"

"You two were close," I mutter.

"Apparently, not close enough. He was going to write me completely out of the will."

"And you couldn't have that."

"No!" He takes a threatening step in my direction. "I don't give a rat's ass about his father's wishes. It was meant to go to me!"

"So you killed him."

He curtly nods. "Before he could file his new living will with the lawyer."

"And where could his new will possibly be found?" Maybe if it can't, I can talk him out of this. Pretend it never happened. Look the other way. Could I do that? Could I keep quiet?

The immediate answer comes to me—no. I can't be the reason he gets away with another crime, the entire town none-the-wiser. They should know who their sheriff is and what an asshole he is. I just wish it didn't end this way.

Reaching into his back pocket, he pulls out a folded piece of paper and waves it around. "Right here. The new will. I bet you didn't get that far into the binder now, did ya?"

I shake my head, feeling like a fool. If I had, I never would have handed over such evidence to Neil's killer. Now, I'm paying that price…with my life. "Why pretend he was still alive?" My voice cracks again as he stuffs the paper in his back pocket and raises the gun to point directly between my eyes.

"Had to keep up the ruse." He shrugs with one shoulder. "You understand?"

I nod vigorously.

"Good. Now there's just the matter of you."

My eyes widen as he takes a step in my direction and then another. Everything I fought for in this new life I've made for myself—a new town, a new home, a new job, a best friend, a boyfriend—comes to the surface. A blink. A flash, so quick it's gone in a second.

Fear spikes in my chest, and I turn and run.

But I don't get far before the gun fires, booming across the pasture, and a sharp stinging punch pierces my upper back. The force of it throws me to the ground, face first, and I gasp while clenching the grass. Warmth seeps across my back, and I'm vaguely aware that it's my own blood. It dribbles across my ribs and soaks the front of my shirt.

I fight for air. Gasp. Wheeze.

I wait for the sheriff to come and finish the job, to put a bullet in my brain, but he never does. It's a shame, really, because the pain is so great, so mind-blazing, that I can't think straight. Think clearly. Think at all.

My grappling for the grass weakens as my body turns cold. Vaguely, I hear a car peel away, and it's then I know I'm alone. Except…something is touching my cheek. Lazily, as if my eyes won't work right, I manage to glance up, and what I see doesn't frighten me. Not this time. This time, it's a comfort.

Touching my cheek is Neil. He's crouched down

217

beside me, as transparent as ever, but his sorrow is evident in the way he holds his eyes, the way he holds himself.

And just as quickly as he was there, he fades, and so does my vision.

CHAPTER 24
COLE GARNER

As I drive over the godforsaken bumpy road, the two shovels I found rattle around in the bed of my truck. It had been a little longer than the ten minutes that I told Tegan I'd be, but hopefully, I'll make up for that fact because I have two shovels instead of one.

Part of my mind still doesn't want to believe that she's being haunted by Neil. But I saw the evidence for myself. I saw the shock on her face, the fear. There's no way she made this up or staged it, and even I have to admit that I saw the petals in random places throughout the house. When she was at Tori's shop, one minute there'd be nothing there, and the next time I looked, there'd be a petal. On the floor. On the counter. Completely random places but always in my path.

At the time, I really hadn't thought much of it.

Tegan's driveway approaches, and just as I'm about to pull onto the gravel, I slam on the brakes. A car is peeling out of it, a cop car, I realize. I scowl as Smith whips his car onto the road, his face ghost-white and his eyes wide. Sitting in the passenger seat, the barrel propped against the window, is a shotgun. As he whips around the corner, it falls over.

Did Tegan find something? Did she call him? If she had, why aren't his lights flashing? And why would he be leaving instead of calling in the cavalry?

A terrible feeling settles in my gut that something is so wrong, forcing him to leave in such a hurry.

Once he's fully on the road, racing away, I pull into the driveway and head toward the house. I remind myself, yet again, that this driveway needs new gravel because all the holes are throwing me around my cab. I can't imagine what Tegan's car is like, trying to make it through this mess.

Parking my truck behind Tegan's car, I hop out and grab the two shovels, one in each hand. If I know Tegan, and based on the fact that Smith was here, she's already in the back, probably deciding her plan of action on how to get the roses out of the way.

I head around the house hurriedly because she just might be crazed enough to try to pull them out by hand. Wading through the tall grass of the backyard, I frown when I don't see her. The barbed wire is half removed, and a portion of the roses is uprooted, but still, no Tegan in sight. Did she go back to the house?

I glance once at the house. Maybe she didn't find anything? Maybe she's waiting for me to get here?

It's a little awkward, but I slide through the fence and make my way to the rose bed, carefully watching my step to avoid a few piles of horse manure. As soon as I get there, though, I stop because anyone would stop if they saw a skull.

"Fuck," I whisper. She'd been right. I glance back toward the house. If she was right, why isn't she still out here? If she's right, why wouldn't Smith still be here? Why wouldn't there be more cops?

As I swivel back toward the grave, I see it. The body in the grass, face down. A head of blond hair. Familiar clothes stained red.

At first, my mind doesn't believe it, but then my heart thuds in my chest, and my stomach sinks to my gut. The breath whooshes from my lungs as though I'd been punched.

True fear cripples me as I throw the shovels to the ground and *run* to Tegan. I drop down beside her, cursing. It doesn't take a genius to figure out what happened here. The gun in Smith's car, the look on his face, the blood all over Tegan. Whether she called him or he came on his own, I don't know, but she showed him the evidence, and he shot her for it.

The only reason he'd shoot her was to hide what truly happened that day that Neil disappeared.

"Tegan," I call, brushing hair from her face. Her back barely rises and falls with each breath, and her eyes are shut. Blood seeps from the corner of her mouth, and my fear skyrockets.

I can't lose another person. I can't!

I whip out my phone and call 9-1-1. As soon as they answer, I prattle off the address, telling them that Tegan had been shot, and then I hang up because, as I watch, Tegan's breathing becomes more shallow.

Gently, I turn her over. She doesn't make a sound

221

as I do, even though it has to hurt like hell. Maybe she's too far gone to feel it? The thought does absolutely nothing to comfort me.

As soon as she's on her back, I tap her cheek. "Tegan, open your eyes!"

A bubbling cough comes from her mouth, and blood gushes out. Her eyelids flutter for a moment, but she can't seem to keep them open.

"Tegan! Open your damn eyes!"

I tap her cheek again, but her head rolls around. My fear intensifies. There's no way an ambulance will make it in time, and there's no way I can get her to the doctor in time either. I don't know anything about injuries like this!

My voice is deep and full of emotion as I gather her to my chest. I cradle her head and rock her back and forth. "Stay with me, sweetheart. Please don't leave. Stay with me."

I listen to her labored, slow breaths as I murmur to her. I tell her what she means to me, about how I can't live without her. Fresh tears fall down my cheeks, and it takes me a moment to realize I'm doing it, but over and over again I'm whispering, "I love you."

And I know it to be true. I feel it in my soul, in the way I'm terrified that she will actually die. I want the last words she hears to be the truth. I love her. I'd do anything for her. I'd trade places and die for her.

The sirens sound in the distance, and I shake her a little. "Help is here, do you hear me? Help is here, sweetheart."

I peer down at her face as the last breath leaves her lungs. "Tegan?" My heart races so fast that it rushes through my ears, drowning out the noise of the approaching ambulance.

Cursing under my breath, I lay her flat and start giving her chest compressions. "Stay with me, damn it," I growl as I shove against her heart.

Vaguely, I'm aware of the ambulance on the property. I hear their doors open, and I shout for them. Sweat gathers down my spine, both from terror and from trying to keep her heart beating. But she just lies there, her head jostling as I shove down on her chest over and over again.

The next thing I know, paramedics are beside me, one barking orders at the other. I keep giving compressions, solely fixed on her heart, hoping she breathes again until someone pulls me away from her.

"We've got it from here," the paramedic says.

I heave for air as if the world doesn't have enough oxygen for me while they lift her up and set her on the stretcher. And then they race away with her, out of the pasture and through a gate that's never used.

At first, I'm frozen to the spot, staring at all the blood soaking the grass. And then, I'm moving, *running* after them. They're loading her into the ambulance when I reach them, but when I try to get inside, a paramedic puts her hand on my chest.

"I'm coming with," I growl at her.

"The cops were closely behind us. They'll be here any minute, and you have to answer questions."

"I'm going with Tegan!" I shout.

The paramedic gives me a sympathetic look. "We've got her."

"But her heart stopped beating!" I look past her

223

and watch as another paramedic is doing chest compressions while another is hanging a bag of blood.

She shakes her head. "We'll try to revive her, but no matter whether you come with or if you stay, the result will be the same."

More sirens sound in the distance, of what can only be the police she promised. I barely register it, though, because saying that her heart stopped beating makes the situation real for me. Tegan is dead. She's dead...

Rage fills me, and the paramedic must see it on my face because she says, "Catch who did this to her, and we'll do what we can for Tegan."

And with that, she shoves me back a little and closes the back of the ambulance door. She jogs around to the driver's side, hops in, and puts on her sirens as she races away.

And then I'm left standing there, my limbs numb but my blood full of pure anger. When the cops arrive, I tell them everything I know. At first, they don't believe me, the word of a murderer against the reputation of a fellow cop, but they jot down everything anyway. At one point, they try to call Smith, but he doesn't answer.

I tell them what I know, how we thought it was Derek, how we handed over evidence that it was, and how Derek and Smith hate each other. I don't have all the answers, but I demand for them to believe me.

When it's over, when they've questioned me to no end, they send me away.

I stomp toward my truck and yank the door open. Hopping in, I immediately roar the engine to life. It doesn't take long for me to get out of the driveway and onto the road, and when I do, I point my truck toward Mount Pleasant.

Tori has no idea that her best friend is dead. She has every right to know, and truth be told, I need to tell someone who will actually believe me.

My mind revisits Tegan's last breath the entire way there, and before I know it, I throw my car into Park in front of Tori's shop. I march my way to her front door and try to open the door, but it's locked.

Growling, I bang on the door. The glass nearly shatters under the force of my fist, but it doesn't take long for Tori to pop her head around the corner of a shelf, a frown on her face. But then she takes me in and races to the door to unlock it.

"Cole?" she greets as she opens the door.

I shove past her and step into the shop, my hands flying to my head. If I had long enough hair, I'd be pulling it out. She's dead. No heartbeat. No breath. She's gone!

"What is all over your shirt?" I whip around to face her, and I don't know what she sees, but her expression flickers from confusion to realization. "Is that blood?" she asks quietly.

"It's Tegan's," I growl.

I watch as she gulps. "What do you mean it's Tegan's?"

I've never been a subtle guy. I've never been one to beat around the bush, and this time, it's no different. "She's dead. Killed."

Her mouth parts, and fresh tears prick her eyes. It's a relief when a sob racks her body because I know she believes me. I don't have to do any convincing that the person we love is gone from this world.

"What happened?" she asks through a sob.

I explain everything, from the realization that Neil was buried under the roses to getting the shovels to seeing Smith. I explain how I found her, and as I do, Tori covers her face and starts crying into her palms.

I wait until her crying subsides, and fresh tears, tears I never shed before today, prick my own eyes. I begin pacing the floor, trying to get them to stop shedding, and as I do, Tori hiccups and asks, "Sheriff Smith did this?"

Pausing in my rage, I turn to face her. "I'm going to kill him," I confess.

She angrily wipes away tears. "Not if I get to him first."

I can tell by her tone that she isn't taking me seriously, so I say, "No, Tori. I'm going to kill him. Hunt him down. Make it hurt."

Taking me in, hearing the conviction in my tone, she crosses her arms over her chest. "Cole—"

I shake my head. "I've killed before, and I have no problems doing it again."

At my confession, her face pales, and it's then that I realize that Tegan never told her the truth. She never told her about my past. I know now that I'll never be able to make it up to her for protecting me.

"If that's true," she begins carefully, "then, not only would you have ended another life, but you'd go back to jail."

I throw my hands in the air. "Do you think I give a

shit? She's dead, Tori! I have nothing and no one left for me!"

"So you're going to avenge her death?" she says through clenched teeth. "Tegan thought the world of you. Do you really think she'd want you back in jail?"

"Tegan would want me to catch the murdering bastard however I saw fit."

Tori uncrosses her arms and holds them wide open. "So hunt him down, but catch him and turn him in. Let him be the one who rots in jail!"

I think it over for a moment. She makes it sound so simple, but my mind wants one thing: Smith's blood on my hands. "I don't know if I can do that—not kill him."

She drops her arms back to her sides. "I don't know everything you've done, she's kept that from me, but clearly, it's a lot. And clearly, she thought you were a changed man. Don't prove her wrong, Cole."

Glancing away, I flex my jaw and curl my fingers into fists. On some level, I know she's right, but another part of me wants to watch him die at my hands. He deserves it, he deserves to feel his heartbeat stop. He deserves to know his time is limited on this earth, and he deserves to question where his spirit will go on his last breath.

"Cole…" she calls to me.

Jaw still flexed, I look back at her. "How do I find him?"

Sighing, she wipes a stray tear from her eye and says, "Have you tried his house?"

"I came straight here." I shake my head. "But I know he won't be there."

For a moment, her eyes search the ground, and then she's moving. I follow her back into her office, where she sits down in an office chair and wheels it to her desk. She fires up her laptop, and her fingers fly across the screen.

"What are you doing?" I ask after a moment.

"Seeing if he has family where he can hide out."

I shake my head again. "I killed his only family."

She glances up at me, questions in her eyes, but she goes back to her computer when I don't elaborate. "Then other properties he might own."

"He owns a cabin in the woods," I suggest. I remember him saying so to Tegan, inviting her there, in fact. "Ashley Forest."

A few more button clicks and she grabs a piece of paper and starts scribbling on it. When she's finished, she looks at me skeptically and reluctantly hands it over. "This is the cabin's location."

"Thanks," I mutter as I take it.

Turning, I start to head out of the office when she calls at my back, making me halt for a moment. "Do the right thing, Cole. Be the man Tegan thought you were."

My shoulders stiffen, but I don't answer her. Instead, I head out of the shop.

CHAPTER 25
COLE GARNER

S moke is coming from the cabin's chimney as I stride up to it through the trees, telling me that he—or someone—is definitely inside. I had parked down the road and trekked the rest of the way on foot, knowing that he'd hear the roar of my engine if I parked closer.

The cabin isn't large, but it looks like a traditional cabin, made of wood, a large awning, a small back porch, and smaller-than-average windows. The trees are so close to the cabin that they practically embrace it.

Somewhere close by, I hear a twig snap, and I grin a little. I didn't come alone, and I know exactly who is in the shadows, watching for what happens next. One man, a cop whose name I haven't had the chance to even learn, steps out from behind a tree and gives me a nod. I nod back, and he dips behind the tree's shadow again.

All the tweed curtains are drawn on the house, so I

can't see inside any of the windows. But I know he's here, and as I round the back of the house, my suspicions are confirmed because there, parked in the small lot, is his cop car.

I know I can't walk through the front door. That would be stupid. Instead, I head to a window on the side of the house. Carefully, quietly, I test to see if it's unlocked. By some miracle, it is, and it slides open with ease.

Within seconds, I'm inside, squatting in a bedroom and listening to the crackle of the fire from the living room. At this point, I don't care what happens next as long as justice reins down on Smith. I don't even care if I die too, but I'm taking this bastard with me. We can rot in hell together.

My feet are silent as they tread across the wood floor. The bedroom door is open, so at least I won't have to deal with the sound of hinges and latches. I steadily make my way out of the room and down the short hallway, following the sounds and smells of the fireplace.

Once I reach the living room, I spot Smith right away. He's crouched in front of the fire, murmuring something to himself that isn't loud enough to hear above the crackling flames. Resting against the wall, a few feet from him, is the shotgun.

I had come unarmed. Because I'm an ex-convict, it's against my parole to own one. But there are other ways to get the job done than by using a gun.

"Is that what you killed her with?" I say clearly as a greeting.

In the crouched position, he whips around. The

binder lies at his feet, and I recognize a few papers from it burning in the fire. As soon as he sees me, however, he jumps for his shotgun, scrambles with it for a moment, and then points it at me.

A normal person would be afraid, but today isn't normal. Today isn't like every other day.

"How did you find me?" he asks.

I only shrug. "It wasn't that hard. You're predictable, Smith."

"Get out, or I'll kill you!" he shouts.

Stuffing my hands into my pockets, seeming at ease, I rock back on my heels for a moment. "Like you killed your stepbrother? Like you killed Tegan?"

Even though the room is only lit by the fireplace, I can see his face pale. "I should shoot you anyway."

"Why?"

"Because you murdered my cousin. An eye for an eye, Garner."

I hold up a finger. "First, tell me why you did it. Why did you kill your stepbrother?"

Spittle flies from his mouth as he explains the will. "He was leaving me with nothing!"

I shake my head a little. "Then why not kill Derek instead of Neil? There'd be no one left to hand it all over to but you."

His eyes narrow. I can tell he hadn't thought of that at the time.

"That bastard just won't die," he grumbles.

My scowl matches my thoughts as I try to understand what the hell that means and draw up nothing. "What are you talking about?"

"I'm trying to kill him!" he shouts. "Derek just won't die!"

And then it hits me—this mysterious illness that Derek seems to have—and my face relaxes as soon as it does. "You're poisoning him."

His jaw flexes once as he clenches his teeth. "Every damn visit."

"Tea?"

He curtly nods.

"Three murders." I blow out a whistle. "And here I thought I was the one with a one-way ticket to hell."

He blubbers as if he doesn't like to be labeled and on the same level as me. "You'll have two murders if you succeed in killing me!"

"Oh, I'm not going to kill you, Smith."

His nostrils flare as he frowns. "Isn't that why you're here? To avenge your little girlfriend's death?"

"I am avenging her death, but it's not me you're going to answer to for every crime you just confessed to."

He wildly searches the room, looking for an attacker in the shadows. He isn't wrong to do so.

I pinch the microphone cord hidden under my shirt and bring it up to my mouth. "He's armed," I say into the microphone, to the men who are waiting in the trees outside.

I had taken Tori's advice and went to the police station after we talked. They set me up with a microphone. At first, they wanted to prove me wrong, but after the admission just now, there's no way they can deny how right I really am.

One minute, it's just me and Smith, a standoff with a gun in the middle, and the next, the room is swarmed by the same police force he had under his wing. I step back as they shout, guns aimed, for him to put down his shotgun. A smirk plays on my lips when he eventually does, and the smirk grows into a wide grin when they cuff him.

"You're a real bastard, Garner," he spits as they lead him out the front door.

I say nothing as I watch him go. I may not have had the chance to watch him suffer, but a cop behind bars? The inmates will do that for me. Knowing that his suffering will begin the moment he steps foot in prison and until the day he dies gives me a sort of satisfaction that I didn't think possible.

"Cole?" Derek calls as he steps through the front door, weaving between cops to get to me.

"Did you hear that?" I ask as he coughs into his hand. "He's been poisoning you."

"Yeah, yeah," he says, waving his hand in the air. I frown at his dismissive gesture. I thought he'd be more pissed, filled with rage just like I am. "I'll admit myself to the hospital soon, but I was told to come and get you."

"For what?" I grunt. I hadn't thought about what I'd do after proving Smith guilty, but right now, a bottle of whiskey to drown my sorrows seems right. I have nothing left. Nothing. Everything I've ever cared about has been stolen from me.

"Tori wants you at the hospital."

"Why?" *There's nothing there for me but a shell of what Tegan was. A body. A reminder of the fact that I*

233

couldn't protect her and, even worse, that I couldn't save her.

"She didn't say, but I can guess." He rests a hand on my shoulder and gives it a squeeze. "Don't make her do this alone. You both need someone today."

I nod once, my jaw tight. Tori is the only piece of Tegan that I have left. And even though the thought of looking at Tegan on a slab, lifeless and cold, makes me feel like I've been knifed, I can endure it. I can say my final goodbyes. I can ask for forgiveness with the hopes that Tegan is still watching, lingering to hear it.

He gives me a sad smile and releases my shoulder. "I can give you a ride if you want. The hospital is quite a distance, and in your truck..."

I nod once again, not trusting my voice because, now that Smith is arrested, I have to face the truth.

CHAPTER 26
COLE GARNER

The whole way to the hospital, I didn't say a word. Derek tried talking to me a few times, but I never answered, so he more or less was talking to himself after a while between fits of coughs. I'm surprised he stayed on the road with how hard he was coughing, but at least he knows the truth now. At the hospital, he plans to admit himself and let the doctors do the rest.

Hopefully, they can reverse the damage Smith has done. I may not like Derek much, but I don't want him to die either. Smith has a lot to answer for, and I just hope the justice system doesn't fail me like it did in the past.

Instead of answering him, I stared out the passenger window, watching the world go by. The world looks entirely different, less colorful and more gray. Less full of life even.

As we pull up to the hospital and park, I stare at the tall building. They tried to make it futuristic with stone and metal architecture, but as soon as you walk through those doors, you're either greeted with life or embraced by death. There is no in between.

Somewhere in there, my girl's body lies. It makes me want to throw up. It makes me want to run away, and I don't like to run from anything. But unlike my sister, I get to say goodbye, and I won't turn that away because I know I'll regret it. I'll never be able to live with myself. I'm not stuck behind bars that prevent me this time. The only thing preventing me is my own crippling grief that makes it difficult to draw breath.

"Ready?" Derek asks when I just sit there, staring out the front window.

No, I want to say. It's on the tip of my tongue, but I know I have to do this. For me. For Tegan. For Tori. So instead, I hop out of his truck. I hear him sigh as he shuts the door, but he meets me at the front of the truck, and we stride to the hospital entrance together.

"One of the cops told me."

"What?" I ask.

"I don't blame you, you know," he goes on, mid-stride.

I glance over at him. He could blame me for many things, so for clarification, I grunt, "What are you talking about?"

He keeps his gaze facing forward. "For blaming me for my brother's death. For thinking I did it." I say nothing, so he prattles on. "I would have thought the same thing. Neil and I never got along; there's evidence to attest to that. And although I have nothing to thank you for except finding his killer and my almost-killer, I just wanted you to know that I don't blame you."

I grunt again as we enter the hospital. Hospitals have a certain smell that always puts my hair on end. That sterile aroma, the one that seems to remind me that this place is filled with equal amounts of happiness and sorrow. But I shove it aside, and we head to the front desk. I have no idea where Tegan's body is, and Tori is nowhere in sight. She's probably with Tegan, I realize. I shouldn't have expected her to wait for me.

The nurse is on the phone, and she holds up a finger, says a few more things through the receiver, and hangs up. "Can I help you?" she asks us.

My mouth goes dry, and I just stare at her. How do I ask to see my dead girlfriend? How do I ask where they keep dead bodies?

"He's here to see Tegan Adams," Derek says clearly, gesturing with a pointer finger at me. "I'm here to admit myself."

She raises an eyebrow at him, but then she looks at me. I don't know what she sees in my expression because I've never had a mirror to see what grief looks like on me, but she gives me a sad smile and directs her attention to her computer. After a few clicks on her keyboard, she squints at the screen. "She's still on the third floor. Room 308. You'll have to hurry, though. They plan on moving her soon."

Flexing my jaw, I nod once at her. So they haven't moved her to the morgue yet.

"Elevator is just down the hall," she adds, pointing and then turning her attention to Derek.

I don't listen to what he says to her as I stride away on seemingly numb legs toward the direction she said. Once I'm inside the elevator, and thankfully, alone, I jab the button for the third floor. The elevator rises, and I take deep breaths through my mouth. What will Tegan look like dead? I saw her draw her last breath, but hours after her last breath? I saw her alive and vibrant and so full of life. I touched her, kissed her, laughed with her. Became a man I didn't think I'd ever be. That's all gone. She's gone. And she took half of me with her.

Before I'm ready, the elevator door dings and slides open. I swallow thickly and step through. It doesn't take long to find the room her body is in, and I hover just outside, listening to what can only be Tori sniffling inside.

Flexing and unflexing my hands, I step inside.

A wall stands in the way. I can only see Tegan's feet resting on the bed, and standing at the end of the bed, swiping away tears, is Tori. She doesn't notice me at first, not until I call her name.

She immediately rushes to me and throws her arms around my shoulders, knocking me back a step. My shirt dampens as fresh new tears are shed from Tori's eyes, and she begins to blubber on with unintelligible words. I just pat her back because that's all I can do. There's no comfort today, not for me. Nothing can make this feel better.

When her sobs subside, she pulls away and uses her shoulder sleeve to wipe away the mess on her face. "What took you so long?"

"I wanted to be part of catching Smith," I admit quietly.

She nods a little and crosses her arms loosely over her chest. "Well, I'm glad you didn't kill him, but Tegan needs you."

"Tegan is dead," I say, my throat crackling with heavy emotion. Saying it out loud just makes it too real, but I'm not wrong. A dead body is a dead body.

Her eyes narrow and then widen. "No one told you?"

I scowl through a few tears. "Told me what?"

A small smile plays on her lips, and she grabs my hand and tugs me past the wall. I stop as soon as the wall is out of the way and Tegan comes into view. My heart skips a beat at the same time a monitor records hers. Her heartbeat. Her monitor.

She's alive?

Her eyes are closed, and tubes are sticking out of her mouth, a machine pumping air into her lungs. Her hair is a mess around her head, and what was once a creamy pallor of skin is now ash white and sickly, but… "She's alive?" I whisper.

I'm vaguely aware of Tori nodding. "They got her heart beating again in the ambulance. The bullet hit her lung, and they were able to remove it. She's still in critical condition, but they think she'll survive it. They plan to move her to the ICU here soon."

"Then why isn't she awake?" I ask as I shuffle closer to the bed. My heart thuds incredibly fast, so fast that I can feel it in the pulse of my neck. My mind just won't fully commit to the fact that she's alive, but my entire body pricks with awareness. *With relief.*

I brush a stray hair off Tegan's face. She's not as cold as I expected her to be, but she looks so helpless, so fragile hooked up to everything.

"They put her in a coma, but it'll only be for a few days."

"Why?" I ask quietly.

"They want her body to rest," she answers just as softly.

I take in Tegan's face as I settle on the bed beside her. I fold her hand in mine and say more for myself than for Tori, "But she'll live."

"She'll live. Well, as long as she doesn't try to die on us, anyway." I hear a little humor in her voice, but I can tell that it's fake. She's just trying to lighten my mood, but she doesn't know that she doesn't need to. I feel on top of the world, and if anyone can pull through this—if anyone can out-stubborn death—it's Tegan. That's just the way she is and will always be.

"If I would have killed Smith..." My voice trails off as my thoughts head to the unthinkable.

"Then you would have truly lost Tegan forever. Jail isn't good for relationships."

I glance back at her and observe her hard expression. "Thank you," I say with complete conviction.

A surprised look widens her eyes. "For what?"

"For convincing me not to kill him."

"Oh." She touches her cheek as if it itches. "You're welcome."

I look at Tegan again. If I had killed Smith, Tegan would have never forgiven me. She'd want me to exact revenge, sure, but not in the way of ending someone's life. Tegan doesn't like death, and though she understands why I killed someone before, she knows I'm not a helpless child anymore. I'm an adult, and an adult with evidence that can't be ignored. If I did away with the law and took it into my own hands, I'd have no excuses. I'd rightfully go to prison, leaving her alone.

We may not be solving murders anymore, but I'll never leave her alone again because I got a taste of what it was like to lose her. To feel a part of myself die with her. And I vow, right here, right now, that it'll *never happen again.*

CHAPTER 27
TEGAN ADAMS

What is that beeping? A steady electronic beeping slithers into my ears and grows louder the more conscious I become.

Why is my hand cold? I lazily flex that hand and feel a sharp sting. When I hiss between my teeth, I end up groaning because doing that simple act made my chest hurt.

"Tegan?" a deep voice rumbles.

I squeeze my eyes shut because they're dry as hell and then try to pry them open. It takes more effort than I care to admit, but eventually, they listen, and the face to the voice blurs into focus.

Cole.

I try to sit up and end up groaning again.

"I wouldn't recommend moving," he says, and dare I say it, there's a small smile on his face. But in his eyes…are his eyes watery?

"What happened?" I croak out. "Where—"

He reaches over and grabs something. "Drink

this," he says, bringing a straw to my lips. Wrapping my lips around the straw, I take grateful swallows as he answers me. "You were shot. You're in the hospital."

I stop drinking as soon as the memories slam into my thoughts. The rose petals, the roses, the skull, the barrel of the gun, the sound of it going off, and a sharp punch to my back. The soft caress to my cheek as the world faded away. Neil Wordon's face.

"Sheriff Smith," I hoarsely say.

"Arrested," he nearly growls as he sets the cup back on a stand that's out of my view. I watch as his face hardens in anger.

Shakily, I raise a hand and touch my dry lips. "Good," I whisper because talking hurts too damn much. I lower my hand to my throat, trying to massage it.

He gently takes my hand and folds his fingers between mine. "They put you in a coma for a few days. You had a ventilator breathing for you, and the doctor said it'll hurt for a while."

As if called upon, someone knocks on my hospital room's door. We both glance in that direction as a man in a white lab coat walks in. His head is completely shaven, but he has a black goatee wrapped around thick lips and a narrow chin.

Smiling, he proclaims gently, "You're awake."

I nod. "When can I go home?" Even though, in what feels like another lifetime, I wanted to work in a hospital and be a coroner, all hospitals hold for me now are bad things. Horrible memories. Excruciating experiences. I want nothing more than to leave.

"Oh." He blows out a breath and stops beside my bed. Stuffing his hands into his lab coat's pockets, he adds, "Let's give it a few days, hmm?"

I drop my head back on my pillow and wince, immediately regretting it. "How long was I out?"

"Three days," both the doctor and Cole say.

I scowl. "That's a long time."

"It gave you time for your lung to heal," the doctor explains. He lifts my other hand and checks the IV. When he's satisfied, he gently sets it back down. "You're a lucky girl, Ms. Adams."

"How lucky?" I ask, swiveling my gaze between Cole and the doctor.

"You were dead." Cole's voice cracks on the last word.

Dead? I turn my attention to the doctor with wide eyes. "For how long?"

"It doesn't matter." He waves me off. "They got your heart beating again in the ambulance and made quick work of getting you here. What matters now is that you're going to be fine."

Satisfied with that answer, I give him a nod and squeeze Cole's fingers for the support I know he needs.

The doctor excuses himself after checking my vitals, leaving Cole and me alone. He's having a hard time looking at me, so I ask softly, "Who found me?"

I watch as he swallows with difficulty, still avoiding my gaze. "Me."

Shit. I slowly exhale, knowing that had to be hell on him. By his pained expression, I know I'm right. "I'm sorry."

His brows pinch together, but his eyes meet mine. "You're not allowed to die."

I chuckle a little and wince again as I do. "My therapist once said that everyone dies and we should just accept it. I'm starting to think he was an asshole."

His expression becomes serious. "I mean it, Tegan. I love you, and if we're going to make this work, you cannot die before me."

My breathing stops for a second, and I study him as his words sink in. *Wait...* "You love me?"

I'll give him credit, he doesn't break eye contact. I know those words, those feelings, are foreign to him, so for him to be so sure, to say it the way he had, he means it.

"I do."

The smile that spreads across my lips grows into something so wide that my cracked lips ache. "What would you do if I said I love you too?"

"Die a happy man," he grunts.

I bring our joined hands up to my mouth and press a kiss to his knuckles. "Let's not talk about death anymore. But I mean it, though. I do love you."

Satisfied with that answer, he sits on the side of my bed, mindful not to jostle me, and leans down. He's careful when he kisses me on the lips, and against them, he whispers, "I've been dying to do that since the moment I found out you were alive."

I chuckle underneath him. "What stopped you?"

He shrugs a little, but there's a ghost of a grin on the corners of his lips. "The tubes, mostly. But Tori, secondly."

I frown a little. "Where is she anyway?" It's unlike her not to hover and fret.

"The shop. It opened the other day, but she said something about being here tonight."

Nodding, I settle back a little into my pillow, and he presses a kiss to my eyebrow before leaning away to sit upright. "What now?" I ask, sore but content.

"What do you mean?"

"Where do I go from here?"

That brilliant grin of his appears, and it's then I realize how much I missed it. With the seriousness before my incident, it had been absent. "I have a few ideas, sweetheart."

"Care to share?" I press with a raised eyebrow.

He shakes his head, and I know then that he's up to something, but as always, he's going to refuse to tell me until the time to do so arrives. That's fine. I got my life back. This new life I didn't think I'd ever have, having it almost stolen from me, and then reclaiming it? I feel lucky. I feel on top of the world. And I feel like I have the whole future ahead of me. It's a future that I know, without a doubt, involves the man in front of me, and absolutely *nothing* could make me happier.

If we can survive death, then I feel sorry for what the universe throws at us next. I am not afraid.

CHAPTER 28
COLE GARNER

The truck jostles a little as we pull into the cemetery. It looks entirely different during the day than at night. The stones' smooth surface glares under the rays, and the short grass sways in the breeze.

With the truck windows down, I can smell the sweet scent of wildflowers at the edge of the lot. The small mountains are more visible under the sun, and truth be told, it's an even more breathtaking place for a final rest than I figured before.

As the truck hits another hole, Tegan curses a little while clutching the two roses, one in each hand. I wince because, even though she was released from the hospital today, she still has to be in pain. "Sorry," I mutter.

"It's okay," she answers, but I can hear the pain in her voice. "They really need to redo more than half the roads in this town."

I grin a little at that because she isn't wrong. I'm just glad she's alive to say it.

The last few days at the hospital were smooth sailing. That is all except Tegan's dire need to be released. The doctor wouldn't budge on that though, no matter how many times Tegan begged. She had a major trauma to her chest, and he wasn't about to let her out of his sight. I didn't say it out loud, but I completely agreed with him.

I stayed with her every day and each night, only leaving to shower and change clothes. Because I've barely stretched my legs, I'm feeling a little restless. I'm sure she feels the same.

As soon as we stepped foot out of the hospital, she demanded to go meet my sister. It must have been how close she was to death that compelled her desire to do such a thing, to visit the grave of someone long dead. Or maybe, since my sister was a big part of my life, she wanted to know that side of me as well. We had talked about my past several times while she rested in her hospital bed, each topic more uncomfortable than the last, but I'm done hiding things from her. I love her, and I want her to love every part of me, even the ghosts that haunt me from my past.

Something tells me she can chase those ghosts away.

When we've reached our destination, I park the truck and look over at Tegan. I eye each rose and grunt, "Are those really necessary?"

"Yes." She scowls at me. "We've talked about this, Cole. It's what you do, bring flowers to graves of loved ones."

"But they're dead."

She chuffs. "You and I both know that dead doesn't always mean *dead*. She could still be watching."

I grunt as I grab the door handle, hop out of the truck, and head to the passenger side. There's no point in arguing with her. If she's compelled to do this, then I'll stand watch while she does.

I'm careful to help her out of the cab, making sure she doesn't have to make unnecessary movements that could cause her pain.

The breeze makes her hair float about her face, and the sun shines on her creamy skin. Just a few days ago, that skin looked ashen, close to a corpse.

"Where's she at?" Tegan asks as we round the truck and dip into the rows of tombstones.

Without responding, I lead us to my sister's grave and then stuff my hands into my pockets when we stand before it. A slow breath leaves her lungs while I hold mine in, waiting for her to say something, anything, to make the ache in my chest go away.

"Bethany Ann Garner," she reads. She glances at me, reading the pain in my expression, and adds on a whisper that the wind catches, "That's a beautiful name."

I nod once, not trusting my voice. And I think she knows that standing before my sister with the woman I love is almost too much to handle because she doesn't ask me any more questions. Instead, she steps forward and lays one rose on the flat surface of the top of the stone.

She hovers there for a moment, hand pressed

against the rose, before she speaks, and it's not to me. "I'm sorry I never got to meet you, Bethany." My heart twinges. "I'm sorry how horrible your life was, but everyone who wronged you is either dead or put away, thanks to your brother. He protected you. And I know that you may not be around, listening to me prattle on, but I just wanted you to know that I'll take care of him. I'll see to it that he is loved and that he laughs, and I hope you can rest in peace knowing that."

I look up at the sky, forcing a few tears to disappear by blinking rapidly. No one has ever cared enough for my sister, no one except me. But Tegan's words touched something inside me, caressed the grief to soothe the wound. I don't know if she'll ever know how much that simple speech means to me.

When she's finished, she comes to me and wraps her free hand around my middle. "From what you told me, I think your sister and I would have gotten along well."

I tip my head back down to tuck her head against my chest and kiss the top of her hair. "You would have." All she ever wanted for me was a life better than what we had, to see the world differently than something so dark and twisted. To have a life outside of protecting her. I was so serious, and all she wanted was for me to smile. And now I have all that with Tegan.

All too soon, she pulls away and begins moving to a freshly dug plot a few rows over. I know where she's going—we discussed it when we bought the roses—so

I dutifully follow her until she comes to a stop by the grave.

Neil Wordon's name is etched across the stone. His brother had his face engraved against the surface. It was a nice touch, even for someone who hated him.

"May you rest in peace, Neil," she murmurs as she sets the second rose on top of his stone just like she did for my sister.

"Do you think he actually is?" I ask.

She looks over her shoulder at me. "Is what?"

"Resting in peace? Gone from this world and on to a better place?"

The breeze gusts for a second, shoving her hair into her face. She pushes it back while she answers through a smile, "Yes." She says it in a way that she knows for certain, and who am I to disagree with her? It wasn't me who he was haunting. It was her. They shared some kind of bond from the afterlife, so if she thinks he's gone, I'm going to believe her.

I stuff my hands into my pockets and nod. She turns back to look at the stone for a long while, and when she's done, she heads back to me, grabs my hand, and we stroll back to my truck.

"Where now?" she asks as I help her into the cab.

"I thought we'd get some donuts."

A slow smile spreads across her lips. "You know me too well."

I grunt, but I can't help the smirk. The door hinges creak as I slam it shut, and the breeze pushes at my back until I'm hopping inside and sliding behind the wheel. I start the truck, and we head back into town.

"Tori said something to me while you were getting

251

my going-home clothes this morning," she begins tentatively.

I glance at her. "Yeah?"

She nods, and I look back at the road. "The sheriff's story was in the paper. All of it. All of his crimes. Have you read it?" I shake my head. "The town knows about it now. They know why you did what you did to Sheriff Smith's cousin."

My grip on the steering wheel tightens at the same time my jaw flexes. A part of me is protective of that story. A part of me doesn't want them to know that part of the truth because that means I have to share a piece of my sister's horrible fate. And then the other part of me is grateful because they know what kind of assholes I was faced against.

"They understand, you know," she says softly when I say nothing. "Why you killed the sheriff's cousin. Tori said the whole town is talking about you, and it's all good things. They're angry that they weren't given the truth, that they couldn't defend their youth when you needed it most."

I flex my fingers that were gripping the steering wheel. "It doesn't change the past, Tegan."

"No," she whispers. "But it does change the future."

Knowing she isn't wrong, I give a nod. She's asking me to step into the future with her, to let go of my painful past and walk a new path beside her. She's asked something similar of me before, but I wasn't ready to let it go. That was before I knew I loved her. That was before I envisioned what comes next between her and me. And that was before she died in my arms and my world stopped for a day. It's a lesson. A lesson that life is too short and I should embrace the blessings I have now and not the curses I was once plagued with.

When we get to the shop, I help her out of the truck again. "Wow," she says as soon as I set her on her own two feet. "There are a ton of people here for the middle of the day."

I hide my grin behind her back as I lead her into the shop. Cheers erupt right when we open the door, startling Tegan and causing her to bump slightly into my chest.

Thanks to Tori, everyone showed up: the police force, Derek Wordon, the cashier from the hardware store, anyone whose life Tegan has touched. Tori organized the whole thing yesterday, a welcome-home party. A celebration of catching Neil's killer.

She looks back at me with wide eyes and asks, "What is this?"

"It's for you!" Tori exclaims. She comes forward, snatches Tegan's hand, and pulls her deeper inside.

"A party?" I hear Tegan hiss as I follow behind them.

"Exactly," Tori answers, guiding her to the police force, where each of them shakes her hand. They pepper her with questions about her medical condition, all of which she dutifully answers. A few times, one by one, they make eye contact with me and give me a curt nod. An acceptance, I realize after a while. A mutual respect. An understanding.

Maybe Tegan wasn't wrong. Maybe the people are on my side, and I'm no longer that murderer, the black stain on this sleepy little town. I don't know what to make of it, so I just nod back.

After Tori has shown her to everyone, she takes us to the booth where Derek sits. He was released from the hospital yesterday, and already, the color is returning to his skin, and the dark circles under his eyes are less prominent.

We take a seat beside him, and he smiles at us while toying with the rim of his coffee cup. "Life looks good on you, Tegan," he says.

"Thanks," she responds, wincing a little as she adjusts her posture.

"Still in pain?" he asks with a raised eyebrow.

I answer, "Yes," at the same time she lies and says, "No."

Frowning at her, I add, "We won't be staying long. She needs to rest."

"I'm fine," she grumbles.

"You are not," Tori interjects, patting Tegan on the shoulder gently. "Normal people aren't fine after they are shot in the back."

Tegan wrinkles her nose at her best friend, and Derek chuckles a little. Then, he digs into his pocket and pulls out two envelopes. I know exactly what those are, and I suppress a grin as the rest of Tori's and my plan unfolds.

Derek hands her one envelope and me the other. "What's this?" Tegan asks as she takes it.

"The reward," he grumbles as though passing over that amount of money was painful for him. It probably was.

"For?"

254

"Catching Smith," I answer.

Derek sighs and rests his chin in his hand while he glances at the envelopes longingly. "You both caught him; you both deserve it. I split the reward in half."

She blinks rapidly, opens the envelope, and her eyes go wide as she reads the amount. "Holy shit."

"I know," he whines.

I chuckle under my breath and then look at Tori. "Is it done?"

Her grin is wide, and Tegan swivels her gaze between Tori and me. "Is what done?"

Tori holds up a finger, then digs into her back pocket to grab a folded piece of paper. She opens it, flattens it against the surface of the table, and slides it to her. As Tegan looks it over, Tori explains, "It's the house you loved. The one I showed you at the shop and you said you couldn't afford? Well, now you can. The owners are waiting for your bid."

I didn't think it was possible, but Tegan's eyes grow even wider as she glances up at me and then at Tori. "It's mine if I want it?"

Tori nods, grinning ear-to-ear. "Just give the word, and I'll make the call."

At that moment, Derek's phone begins to ring. He excuses himself, and I slip out of the booth to let him out. As I sit back down, Tegan sheds a tear. She looks at Tori and says, "Yes. Yes, I want the house."

Tori claps and squeals a little. "Okay, I'll call them right now."

She quickly exits the booth with her phone in her hand, leaving Tegan and me alone. She studies me for a moment before asking quietly, "What about you?"

I raise an eyebrow. "What about me?"

"What are you going to do with your money?"

I shrug a little. I hadn't thought about it. "Save it, I guess."

"Are you still going to work?"

"Yeah," I say, nodding. "Derek hired me to oversee all of his rentals as well as finish the renovations."

"And…" She looks down at the house again. "Where will you live?"

"The trailer, most likely." I've never needed anything more than what I have.

She looks at me again, twisting her lips to the side, and I can tell she wants to say something. Finally, she blurts, "Move in with me."

My eyebrows raise high into my forehead. "Move in with you?"

"I know it's soon," she begins quickly, grabbing the paper's edge and swiveling it to face me. "We haven't been dating long, but Cole…we've literally walked through death together. I died. I was dead. And I don't want to waste this second chance. I want to spend every minute with the man I love. I want to go to sleep and wake up with you. I want to joke and argue with you, under one roof. Please, Cole. *Please* move in with me. Please say yes."

It's a no-brainer for me, which is surprising because, if anyone would have told me a month ago that I'd be sharing my life with someone, I would have rolled my eyes. But now? Now, everything is different. I'm different. I'm a better man, thanks to the woman across from me. She's given me my life back. She's given me reason to live. Of course I want the same things she does. So I nod and say, "Okay."

"Really?" she asks, surprised.

I nod again and take her hand in mine. "Yes."

And I mean it because I know, without a doubt, that I'll spend the rest of my life loving her. I'll spend the rest of my life protecting her, making sure she's happy and safe. That life begins now.

I lean across the table and gently press my lips to hers. It begins and ends with her.

Always.

A LOOK AT BOOK TWO
FIELD OF LILIES

Tori

My name is Tori Townsend and I have three problems.

Problem number one: I'm a sucker for the walking red flags.

Problem number two: I never thought I'd kill someone.

The third and worst problem of all and what really takes the cake ... I certainly never thought I'd be hunted.

Killian

I don't like to tell people my full name, just like I don't like to tell people anything about my past. If they knew, they'd do more than steer clear of me because of my rugged appearance.

Drifting. That's what I've been doing, in search of the elusive person who wronged me. The man who took everything from me because of what I did to him.

But when I walked into Fairview, I hadn't expected for all hell to break loose, and I hadn't expected the woman who owns the B&B I've been staying at, the woman who is slowly winning me over, to be in trouble. I just wish it wasn't because of my past.

AVAILABLE JANUARY 2026

USA TODAY Bestselling DV Fischer is a mother of two very busy boys, a wife to a wonderful and patient (thank god) husband, an owner of three sock-loving German shorthairs, and slave to a cat they pulled out of a dumpster (literally), Geralt. Together, they live in Sheldon, Iowa.

When DV Fischer isn't chasing after her children, she spends her time typing like a madwoman while consuming vast amounts of caffeine. Just kidding. She can't do that anymore. One cup a day or she regrets all her life choices for the next twenty-four hours.

Known for the darker side of imagination, she enjoys freeing her creativity through plus-size romance that may only exist between the pages, no matter how much we wish otherwise.

www.dvfischer.com